6/1/22

KT-408-172

WELL AND GOOD

Since the death of their mother in a hit-and-run accident, Violet and Jane have been living with their great-grandfather Luke Grant and his partner Helena. One evening Violet's boyfriend goes missing and is finally found badly injured and unconscious. The police investigation follows the suspects to the island of Madeira and uncovers a bizarre and unscrupulous scam...

Gerald Hammond titles available from
Severn House Large Print

Crash
Hit and Run
Loving Memory
Waking Partners
Keeper Turned Poacher
On the Warpath
Cold in the Heads

WELL AND GOOD

Gerald Hammond

Severn House Large Print
London & New York

This first large print edition published 2010
in Great Britain and the USA by
SEVERN HOUSE PUBLISHERS LTD of
9-15 High Street, Sutton, Surrey, SM1 1DF.
First world regular print edition published 2009 by
Severn House Publishers Ltd., London and New York.

British Library Cataloguing in Publication Data

Hammond, Gerald, 1926-
   Well and good.
   1. Youth workers--Crimes against--Fiction. 2. Detective
   and mystery stories. 3. Large type books.
   I. Title
   823.9'14-dc22

ISBN-13: 978-0-7278-7901-1

Severn House Publishers support The Forest Stewardship Council
[FSC], the leading international forest certification organisation. All
our titles that are printed on Greenpeace-approved FSC-certified paper
carry the FSC logo.

Mixed Sources
Product group from well-managed
forests and other controlled sources
www.fsc.org Cert no. SA-COC-1565
© 1996 Forest Stewardship Council

Printed and bound in Great Britain by the
MPG Books Group, Bodmin, Cornwall.

PROLOGUE

The meeting in Newton Lauder Memorial Hall got under way, only twenty minutes late. Sir Peter Hay was in the chair, not just because he was the wealthiest man for many miles around but also because the meeting was being held at his behest. The attendance was thin but this did not displease him. Nothing else was to be expected on a sunny Sunday afternoon in midsummer, but it meant that those attending were those who were already interested in what he had to say.

Sir Peter blinked as a sudden ray of sunshine found its way inside, made visible by the dust stirred up by the many feet. He was an untidy figure, his grey locks overdue for a haircut, but to lend dignity to the proceedings he had donned his second-best kilt. Nobody noticed. His figure was so familiar in that part of the Scottish Borders that the details were taken for granted.

When he rose to speak there was instant silence. He looked around him affectionately. He was a much-loved figure in the area and in return he regarded all the locals as his personal babies. 'We must all be aware that times are changing,' he said in his rather neighing voice. 'And not necessarily for the better. The police who used to protect our property are now ordered instead to protect the young tearaways who run riot, intimidate our old people and vandalize whatever they don't fancy stealing. The clip round the ear that used to do the job is now classed as common assault and never mind the provocation. The well-intentioned but infamous Human Rights Act has much to answer for.' There was a mutter of agreement.

'All this is in the name of human rights. But though the intention may have been to grant to everybody certain rights, the way it has worked out and has been interpreted, only the lawbreaker scores. We know exactly what's happening. The chances of repealing the act or at least incorporating a clause permitting the victim to give his tormentor a kick up the backside are nil. Nothing so sensible ever finds its way through Parliament in the teeth of those who mean so very well but do so much damage. So we now need to take a step further back and consider the causes – not just why they feel free to misbehave but why they want to do so.

'Many of those present this afternoon are almost as old as I am. There may be one or two who are even older. Like me, they will remember when the business of staying alive took up most of a man's time and energy. Life was an adventure and survival was a triumph. In those days there was little time or energy to spare for putting right the results of bad behaviour, so the concept of good behaviour was instilled as a matter of course. But now, along with a society that no longer penalizes the young wrongdoer and yet protects his belongings, his person and even his identity, we have given that person far more leisure time than ever before without giving him anything to occupy it or showing him how to enjoy it.'

A stout white-haired lady stirred and cleared her throat but Sir Peter soldiered on. Both could tell that it would not be a propitious moment to contradict Sir Peter. He was helping the company to see what they already knew. 'Mrs Robertson is eager to point out the contribution that the District Council has made – the clubs, the football pitches and so on. But unfortunately a boy can not play football for more than an hour or two and attendance at any club soon loses its attractiveness. Playing chess and drinking cocoa are no substitute for the adventure and challenges that were part of the business of living in hard times.

'Let me tell you a story, of sorts, from my own youth,' he said. 'I was often sent away during the school holidays to stay with an uncle in the Neuk of Fife. I spent much of my time mooching around the harbour, seeing what went on, helping when I could and jumping at the chance of a sail whenever it was offered me. Looking around, I could see that the youths of the town were divided. There were boys, mostly the lucky ones who had a father or an uncle to lead the way, who used the time creatively. Time and money were harder to come by in those days but they still managed to come by some craft such as a redundant ship's lifeboat, install an old diesel, build on a cabin and use the vessel usefully and even profitably. They might act as a safety-boat when engineering works were going on, or take out fishing parties or whatever. They were happy and they taught themselves. Later they taught their own children and grandchildren how to use their time and their hands.

'But there was a minority who lacked that help and those facilities, who looked around the boats and said, "Rich man's hobby, let's destroy it." They were the same boys or very similar; they just lacked a starting push. Unfortunately that minority has grown up and taken over and has become a majority by now. These are the youths, or the parents of the youths, who give us the trouble. The rowdies and vandals who simply have no concept of how to make better use of their time and talents except to destroy and have never come to realize what they might achieve if they only made the effort.

'What I want to suggest is that we give them that starting push. There are plenty of retired or still-working men with the skills to guide these youngsters. I can provide premises. The farmer at Kempfield is due to retire. I can offer him a smallholding that would suit him better. The land would be added to the adjacent farm to make a more viable unit. The farmhouse might have a value but farm buildings – barns and cowsheds – without land are a drag on the market. I could make those buildings available to a body such as I envisage, at a peppercorn rent. In my own mind I've been calling that body a Creative Adventure Centre.

'Once the body was up and running I would expect it to provide space, materials and skilled advice to any youngster with a dream. Even the courts might start referring troubled youths to it. But each recruit would be asked, "What do you really want most of all?" The answers would vary but he would be told, "We can provide workshop space and advice and some materials but you have to help yourself. If you want a scrambler motorbike, a skateboard or a paraglider, build it yourself. You may have to earn some of the money for materials, but we can show you how to do that too."

'Some of their aspirations may be beyond all reason but there are always compromises. Suppose that one boy – or girl – says, "I want to build a boat and win the America's Cup." Out of all reason, of course. So we start small. Send him to learn dinghy sailing. Help him to find the materials or the skills to build his own dinghy and work up from there. He may not satisfy his ambition but he'll learn a lot while he tries, about boat-building and navigation, safety and signalling and a hundred other matters.

'Or, a better example, suppose that he

says, "I want to shoot a deer."' There was a small sound of indrawn breath in the hall but most of his audience were following him raptly. Here in the Scottish Borders there was little sentimentality about animal rights. Issues were clearly seen in their own light. Sir Peter resumed, 'We find him a recoverable action and barrel from a rifle whose stock is beyond repair. We start him on fabricating a new stock and refurbishing the action. We put him in the care of a retired keeper or stalker, to teach him ecology and wildlife management. We teach him to stalk, to recognize species of deer and to know their seasons. We teach him about safety and respect for weapons, and about the law. We take him to a range and teach him to shoot. He would have to pass tests on each of those subjects and more besides. Only then is he allowed out on the land in the care of an experienced stalker. By that time, he may no longer want to shoot a deer; he may even be ready to move into wildlife conservation. In such ways we can turn our problem youth around and perhaps even set some of them on course for new careers. We would certainly teach most of them respect for property and give them something to occupy all that surplus time and energy.'

11

Sir Peter coughed apologetically. He was an old man now and public speaking tired him. 'I've given you the gist of it,' he said. 'Before we delve any deeper, I want to know how many here have a skill that they'd be prepared to teach on a voluntary basis. Let's have a show of hands.'

Hesitantly, hands began to go up – first one or two and then more until a dozen or more hands were raised.

'That's very good,' Sir Peter said. 'As I've said, I could make premises available. Premises and skilled guidance together are half the battle already won. The next step will be to appoint a management committee.'

The stout lady, Mrs Robertson, was not going to be denied any longer. 'What Sir Peter has just said has a great deal of sense to it. Whether it could be brought off is another matter, but if you can get it off the ground I can promise you a limited amount of local authority finance.' There was a smattering of applause. Sir Peter, who had expected resistance in that quarter, looked amazed.

A large and heavily built man in dungarees got to his feet. 'There's not many of you will know my face but I'll bet you've seen my name on my lorries a time or two. Jim

Donaldson, Building Contractor, that's me. Now, I suffer from vandalism more than most. A building site in the evenings and weekends is a God-given playground to those wee buggers, begging your pardon, Mrs Robertson. Can't blame them either. They have precious little to do except watch the telly or get up to mischief. But it's my turn to tell you a story. During that last heatwave, a gang of them got into the basement of the new Corsco Building in Kelso. The floor of the substation had been cast, complete with deep channels for the cables to run in. Do you know what they did? They turned on the water and ran a hose and filled those channels with water and when my men caught them they were having a grand time swimming in the channels in cold water. Vandalism, you think? But I wouldn't let the police touch them. It was a clever trick; it gave them something to do in the hot weather and it cost damn little to pump the water away again.

'My point is that boys who could think up that sort of trick and carry it out sensibly without doing any real damage are worth helping and anything that helps them grow up into sensible chiels instead of layabouts sucking on the public tit will get my support. And that's not an empty boast. You'd be surprised if you knew how much good building material goes on the dump or on a bonfire at the end of a contract because it's cheaper to dump it than to sort it and store it and use it again. Before you buy a plank or a nail, speak to me first and I'll find it for you if I can.' He resumed his seat, well satisfied with himself.

Mrs Robertson said, 'Well, that's a very handsome offer, I must say. But I still have a reservation. The mention of rifles and killing deer. The idea of arming these delinquents...'

A lean man got to his feet. His face was half obscured by a month-old beard but what could be seen of it was weather-beaten. 'Maybe we should have left the mention of guns to later, when the project's well in hand and too late to stop. But I'll tell Mrs Robertson to her face that she's looking at it upside down. The men who were brought up near water are never the ones who drown, in the same way that a man who was brought up around guns has learned to respect them, just as Sir Peter said. It's not among the legitimate and trained and licensed gun-users that you must look for the yins as misuse guns. And there's still a proper place and proper uses for them.

'If Mrs Robertson cares, I'll take her out next time we have a long spell of hard weather. I'll show her places where the deer have come down as far as the deer fences in search of food and there they've starved. I'll show her the corpses. It can't be helped. The deer were kept in check by their predator, the wolves. Well, we've wiped out the wolves and we're their only predator now. So it's become our job to control their number so's they don't eat away their habitat. Properly managed stalking is the way to do't, and it brings some money into the district and puts good meat on the market. If I was a red deer I'd rather be given my time on the hill and take my chance on being more crafty than a man with a rifle, instead of being born in captivity and taken to a slaughterhouse the moment there's enough meat on me. So, Mrs Robertson, next blizzard, are you coming with me?'

There was some laughter and some applause. Mrs Robertson reddened. Sir Peter intervened hastily. 'Ask Mrs Robertson again nearer the occasion, Hamish. She'll need a little time to think about it.'

'Nae doubt,' said Hamish. 'Time to consider whether it's politically correct to know the truth or to pretend it's not there.'

Mrs Robertson leaped to her feet as though she'd sat on a wasp. 'I resent that,' she snapped.

'I bet you do.'

Sir Peter rapped on the table before him and there was an immediate silence. 'Plenty of time to debate that issue and a dozen others,' he said mildly. He was hiding a smile. 'For the moment, the fact that views are being expressed is of value in itself, but the place for such debate is in committee. I am shortly going to ask for nominations to a management committee and I intend to begin by nominating both Mrs Robertson and Hamish for membership of it. It will then have to choose its own chairman and appoint a director and a treasurer.'

During the silence that followed, two men at the back of the hall exchanged a look and a nod. Feet began to shuffle on the worn boards and people, mostly men, began to drift towards Sir Peter. There were plenty of volunteers willing to show youngsters how to make this or that, a reasonable quorum willing to serve on the management committee but only the two volunteers required for director and treasurer.

As he went forward to offer his services,

16

Hamish met Sir Peter's eye. He raised his eyebrows a fraction and in return received an almost imperceptible nod. After years in local politics, Sir Peter knew what objections he had to meet and who would make them. Hamish was a plant.

ONE

Three Years Later

The one-year-old black Labrador bitch came out of the gorse at a gallop carrying the red rubber launcher-dummy and presented it, sitting, to the young girl.

'Goody goody gundog,' Jane said, pushing the dummy down on to the spigot. The bitch, Circe, responded to her praise with a restrained wag of her whole latter end. She was panting hard but at the same time grinning happily.

Jane fumbled for another of the tiny blank cartridges and fitted it into the launcher. She held the launcher in a way that would have looked strangely cack-handed to the uninformed bystander – with the launcher pointed away from the thumb so that the kick of the launcher would be taken against the heel of the fist rather than the more vulnerable thumb and fingers. It took her a

19

few seconds to pick out an aiming point where the dummy would land out of the dog's sight. She drew back and released the firing pin. The launcher kicked hard against her fist and the dummy sailed out a good seventy paces, to land in a jungle of bracken. A small flock of sheep in the far corner looked up but disdained to move. Circe had moved forward two paces to where she thought she could mark the fall and then sat tight. Jane praised her but made her wait before sending her to 'fetch'. Circe sprinted out to the general area of the fall but she had been unsighted by the undulation of the pasture. She looked back at her mistress. Jane gave a hand signal and the bitch turned and homed in, picked up the scent and came racing back with the dummy, soaking wet but ecstatic. A fine spring was being followed by a cold, damp summer.

'Goody goody gundog,' Jane said again. It was her favourite expression of the moment. 'But we'd better pack up now. GG says never to go on until you get bored and anyway Roddy McWilliam's coming.' She dropped the heavy launcher and the dummy into a haversack and they set off towards a distant tubular gate. 'We're getting pretty good, you and I,' she resumed. The bitch

was listening, tail working like a metro-
nome, without understanding more than an
occasional word. Tone and body language
were enough. 'We could give them an eyeful
when the season comes round but GG says
that you're too young and it might unsteady
you to meet up with the real thing. You
wouldn't start to run in, would you now? Or
perhaps you would.'

She went on addressing the Labrador
although she knew well that any understanding was vague and patchy. Circe gave
every sign of paying attention, never interrupted and never ever *ever* betrayed a confidence. Secrets were safe with her. They had
the perfect relationship.

The pair passed through the gate and Jane
latched it carefully behind them. A deeply
rutted track led along the edge of a recently
harvested stubble-field. She followed a
coniferous tree strip and then climbed a
stile and plunged into a thick wood. 'Anyway, I want to see Roddy. I don't just mean
see as in *looking at*; I mean that I want a word
with him. Violet thinks he's her boyfriend.
Roddy thinks it too. She may be about a
hundred years older than I am – well, nearly
ten – and he's about two more years older
again, but that doesn't signify. When I'm

eighty he'll only be ninety-two. I think he's very good-looking even if his ears do stick out a bit. Superglue would soon fix that – I don't know why people don't use it and forget about surgery. I want him to show me how to tie a nymph for the trout fishing. GG says that these summery days, when nothing seems to be rising, they're still feeding somewhere and you can get down to them with a nymph or a caddis, he says. That might have done the trick this morning. It was too cold and breezy for flies to hatch.'

The roof of Whinmount was showing through a thin screen of trees. Jane took a seat on a boulder. This was a favourite place of hers, for a respite before going in and losing her individuality by becoming a mere unit in a family.

'Talking of GG, we've lived with him ever since our mum was killed. That was before you were born, of course. The way Mum's will left it, he looks after us until Violet's twenty-one, which isn't so very long now – two years and a bit. No, don't dry your head on me, you daft poopomninc. That means a backward nincompoop, in case you hadn't figured it out. When Violet's twenty-one, which isn't so very long now, she takes over. I'm not looking forward to that – she can get

22

a bit bossy at times. And she takes charge of us if GG pops off or can't carry on any longer before that – you and me both, though you'll still be my dog and don't you forget it.' Recognizing something in her tone, Circe tried to climb into her mistress's lap but was repulsed. 'Down you foul beast! You're soaking wet, and slobbery with it. GG's getting kind of long in the tooth, as they say. Well, he could hardly not, he's my great-grandfather and even given the family tradition of marrying and producing babies young, he couldn't have got there much before being eighty. In fact, he had a birthday not long ago and he was eighty-three, which is really old. Everybody keeps saying how fit he is for his age but he seems to be slowing up, which he's quite entitled to do at that age, but it's very worrying. Sad for him but worrying for me, because if he does find that we're getting too much for him and Violet marries Roddy and I have to live with them I'll feel like a third singer in a duet.'

Rather pleased with the last imagery, she paused for breath and pulled Circe's's ears. 'Just as long as you make up a fourth I'll be OK,' she said. 'But maybe GG would let us stay on with him.'

There was no reply. The Labrador was

staring into up space where sky showed between the treetops. 'You're always doing that,' Jane said. 'What do you see up there? Clouds? Do you ever think that clouds are places too? They may change shape. They may not last for long. They're only water vapour condensed out by the cold high up. But while they're there, they're places. Some day I'll learn to fly so that I can go and visit those places. You can come with me.' She sighed. 'We'd better shift now or we'll be late for dinner.' She began to rise but at her last word the Labrador was up and ready. It was the first word that she had understood.

The house was substantial, at least a hundred and fifty years old but well built and well maintained. It had once been a farmhouse but the farmer had eventually given up struggling against the rocky ground. The house was old, but it had been altered and extended and altered again until the original form was almost lost in what it had become. In such evolutions many houses become a mess but others, like Whinmount, develop character and are loved enough to be preserved from any kind of deterioration.

The principal rooms looked north to the sunlit side of the roofs of Newton Lauder and the hills beyond, but the rooms that comprised the heart of the house had generous windows on to the lawn that was most of the garden. The house had no very near neighbours, being situated in Borders countryside of mingled farmland, forestry and birch woodland.

Jane and Circe circled the house to the front door where they found Jane's sister Violet, wearing a smart summer frock instead of her more customary jeans and jumper, sitting on the teak bench beneath the Virginia creeper and looking fed up, verging on tearful. It was rather cool on the north side of the house but this was the direction from which approaching cars could be seen.

Circe, who rather liked Violet while considering her to be of limited importance, sat anxiously and offered a consoling paw but she was ignored. 'What's wrong?' Jane asked.

'Nothing.'

Jane also had a fondness for her older sister when the latter was not in a bossy mood. 'Come on, now. You don't just sit there looking all soggy and miserable when nothing's happened. Or perhaps you do. Did Roddy stand you up?' she asked hopefully.

Violet drew herself up. 'No,' she said indignantly. 'Well, not what you'd call standing up exactly. But he was supposed to pick me up more than an hour ago. He said he was going to take me out for a meal at that new bistro place. It's only Cagliotti's café with new tablecloths and a drinks license and Tony calling himself a chef instead of a cook, but it's supposed to be very good value. Only Roddy's late and he'll have lost his reservation and I tried phoning his home and his mother said that he borrowed her car and left ages ago, wearing his good suit.'

Jane sat down beside her sister and put an arm round her. There was a strong physical resemblance between the two. Each was slim and straight with a mane of pale chestnut curls. 'Men are like that,' she said, with all the wisdom of a young woman. For most of her young life she had been exposed to the articulate intelligence of her great-grandfather and as a result she was, said her teachers, years ahead of her classmates. 'I wouldn't worry. He's probably met a pal and they've gone off to do boy-things.'

Violet brightened up just a little. 'As long as they aren't doing girl-things I don't mind too much. You don't think anything's happened to him?'

'If you mean an accident, I shouldn't think so. It's only about a mile and a half and there's only one junction. If there'd been a collision his mum would have heard it.'

'He said he might look in at Kempfield on the way.'

'It isn't exactly on the way but it's only a mile or two out of it. But there you are,' said Jane. 'He probably found that his glue hadn't dried or something and he put on a boiler suit, started redoing it and lost track of the time. He'll probably come crawling back begging forgiveness. Will you forgive him?'

'I'll think about it,' Violet said more cheerfully.

'I'd better tell Aunt Helena that you'll be eating with us. And you'd better pray that she hasn't taken out and defrosted three chops.' Circe had been butting Jane with her head, 'All right, Fido, it's your dinner time. I hadn't forgotten.' In point of fact, she *had* forgotten but she was not going to admit it, even to her dog.

They set off round the house to the French windows beside the kitchen. Their feet were too messy for the front hall.

TWO

The evening meal at Whinmount usually passed in a babble of talk. As has been said, Jane, who had lived with her great-grandfather's wisdom and calm logic for many moons, was intelligent far in advance of her years. Luke was always prepared to stop and explain, even about girl things (he had known many women in the fifty-odd years since the death of the girls' great-grandmother) but Jane's chatter often competed with the more adult conversation of the girls' great-grandfather and Helena, the latter's live-in lady friend. Violet, not yet out of her teens, considered herself privileged to join in at whichever level caught her attention.

That day the meal, which was taken in the kitchen, passed in near silence. There was still no message from Roddy. Violet looked longingly at the telephone but it refused to ring and she had too much pride, or was too fearful of what she might discover, to make the first call. She fretted the evening away and, to judge by her looks and yawns at breakfast, slept badly if at all. She looked longingly again at the telephone. The only phones in the house were mobiles. A full mile of overhead wires would be needed to connect Whinmount to the nearest landline and Luke had always jibbed at the cost. But the first ring was at the front doorbell.

Violet began to leap to her feet but then settled back slowly. Roddy must not be allowed to think that she had been worried. 'You go,' she told Jane. Jane, wise beyond her years in matters of dogs and people, did not fully understand the fine shades of behaviour behind the request, but she trotted along the hall.

She was back in a few seconds. 'It's Roddy's mum,' she said.

Violet turned white and looked ready to faint.

Angela McWilliam followed on Jane's heels. Angela had at one time been the life and soul of many a party and at that time she had met Luke Grant. They had had an affair and parted friends. To Luke, she had been one of many. A still vigorous widower living alone for many years, not far from an area of small houses inhabited mainly by widows and divorcees, was bound to have interested many ladies, each of whom cherished the illusion that she had been, if not unique or even a rarity, special. Angela remained blonde, with a little help from the bottle, and she had put on a little weight but only in the most attractive places. Since being left a widow she had become once again the life and soul of parties; but though she had cast an eye in Luke's direction she had decided against trespassing on another's turf. But just let Helena slip up and Angela would fill the gap before Helena could get back on her feet. She had broken off with Luke for the sake of marriage and security, but marriage had been deadly dull and security, now that she had attained it, wasn't all that it was cracked up to be. Her late husband, moreover, had crashed his car while returning over icy roads from a warm and welcoming bed. Luke might be old but there were one or two years of wear in him yet and he had always been a one-at-a-time man. Luke, for his part, had made sure that his own precautions had been successful and that Roddy was not his by-blow. He had then returned his attention to Helena.

Angela arrived in the bright kitchen with a

smile for everybody. It was a smile with a different shade of meaning for each recipient – patronizing for Jane, arch for Violet, conspiratorial for Helena and a special one for Luke. 'Is Roddy here?' she asked.

Luke exchanged a frown for her smile. 'Come in, Angela. Why on earth would you think that Roddy was here?'

Angela's mood took a sudden dive. She settled carefully in the indicated chair. 'When he went out yesterday he was supposed to be meeting Violet. He never came home. What was I supposed to think?'

'Not,' Luke said firmly, 'that he had scored. Certainly not with Violet. I can't speak for the other young ladies hereabouts. Jane, I think you'd better go and tidy your room.'

Thanks to Luke's conscientious attention to the duties of a guardian as he saw them, Jane was well aware of the facts of life and, up to a certain point, their social implications, but she accepted that certain topics were for adults only. Violet would bring her up to speed later. She slipped out of the room.

Violet had turned a becoming shade of pink. She was the picture of confusion. 'I was waiting for him yesterday,' she said. 'He never turned up. We were going to go out for a meal. I can assure you we have never ... would never—'

'Calm down, my dear,' Angela said quickly. 'I had forgotten what a...' She broke off on the point of saying *what a sheltered life you've led*. She also shied away from reminding Luke that he had not always been so concerned about virtue. There is no prude like a reformed rake. '...what a well brought up girl you are,' she substituted quickly. 'What else was arranged between you?'

'Nothing,' said Violet. 'Except that he did say he might call in at Kempfield first.'

'I phoned there. The phone was answered by someone who sounded like a teenager, probably a girl and almost certainly dottled. And I tried to call you here but neither of your mobiles was switched on. He isn't at Kempfield this morning. When he was last there, God knows. He isn't the usual sort to let people down, but most of us,' said Angela, looking Luke in the eye, 'can give way to sudden temptation. He'll probably turn up this afternoon smelling –' once again she edited what she had intended to say '– of beer.'

'You're probably right,' Luke said. 'But I think I'll go and ask a few questions at

Kempfield.' He rose and took his car keys from the sideboard.

'I'll come with you,' Violet said quickly.

Angela stood. 'So will I, if I may. If nothing else, I want to know where my car is. I had to walk here,' she added indignantly. Walking a mile and a half on a cool, sunny morning was, it seemed, beyond her normal capability.

They paused in the hall. 'Give me a moment for a word with Helena and Jane, and then we'll go.'

At the end of the unclassified road where it joined the B-road, they could see ahead of them Birchgrove, the group of smaller houses where the McWilliams lived though there was no entry at that side. If they had turned right they would have descended a long hill that fetched up in the middle of Newton Lauder. Turning left, they were faced with a stiff climb, past the entry to Birchgrove and past also the local hospital.

Luke's Terios crested the last rise. Angela had tried to claim the front passenger seat but the car was small and space limited so Luke had persuaded her that she would have more room in the back. With the slender Violet beside him he had adequate elbowroom.

Emerging from the valley somewhere above and behind the hospital they were on to rolling moorland. Some of it was given over to heather, mostly good for little but grouse and blackgame; but in sheltered and fertile pockets the surviving farms still worked; their sheep, in limited numbers, were welcomed on the moors, opening up paths where grouse could bask or feed. The open moorland was broken by scattered birch woodland and occasional stretches of forestry plantations.

Luke turned off the B-road onto an unusually well-surfaced farm road. The rambling buildings of what had once been Kempfield Farm were ahead of them. To either side, fields were under cultivation or furnished grazing for sheep. The buildings had mostly been reroofed in corrugated metal with broad rooflights and solar panels. Buildings that had once been open-fronted were closed in with glazed screens set in corrugated panels or cedar boarding. The mixture of materials was a result of avail-ability but careful selections had resulted in an overall arrangement that pleased the eye. Rather than looking haphazard, it looked like the thoughtful design of an eccentric architect. Most of the alterations were carried out before application was made for Change of Use, thus bypassing any possible objections from the planning authority.

'My goodness!' Angela said. 'This has come on a lot in the last couple of years.'

'It has,' Luke agreed. 'Sir Peter bequeathed the buildings to the organization, subject to certain conditions all of which have already been met. The first years were a struggle – I'm on the steering committe so I remember them well. But we had some support straight away from the more far-sighted businesses and as soon as they saw that the rougher element was being kept too busy to kick up hell most of the others wanted to jump on the wagon. We have a builder, in particular, who always makes his surplus materials available for our improvements; and the word went round that any boy vandalizing that builder's projects would have to answer to some very tough cookies. They're the ones who are building that,' he added, as they rounded a corner and a large yacht under construction came in view. The framework looked complete and the carvel planking was about up to the waterline. Four young men in overalls were working on it.

Luke drove under an archway and into an extensive courtyard where several cars and some motorbikes were parked. Angela was out of the car like a greyhound leaving the trap. She homed in on an undistinguished grey Volkswagen. 'This is my car but the keys aren't in it. I have the spares with me. But where's Roddy?'

'We'll go and see.' Luke led the way across the courtyard. He was a tall man but the passage of time had given him a gnome-like look. This overlaid the piratical appearance of his strong features, which was accentuated by the eyepatch that he often found more comfortable than his artificial eye. 'The next phase is to roof over here when funds permit. That will give us a bigger workshop for woodworking so that projects like that boat can happen indoors. The metal workshop can inherit the present woodwork shop and its present space becomes storage. This way.' He walked with a limp. Angela, who was hugely uninterested in the future of the buildings, was ahead of him.

Just inside a pair of big doors was a tidy office. The desk supported two books. Luke consulted one and then the other. 'Roddy was here for an hour yesterday afternoon,' he said. 'I don't know what he's making at the moment. He may have been assembling circuit boards. He signed out at about five thirty.'

Angela stepped closer. 'That's when he should have been arriving at your house. Let me see his writing.'

'It won't help you much. They sign in and out by membership numbers. Some of them have handwriting you can hardly make out and their signatures are just a scribble. I had to look up Roddy's number, which is one-oh-six-three. Numerals don't give many clues to handwriting unless the writer crosses his sevens or does something else distinctive. And it's quite usual and permissible for someone to sign somebody else out. The person leaving may have greasy hands or be in a tearing hurry.'

Luke spoke absently. He had seated himself comfortably behind the desk and was comparing numbers in the two books while making notes on a page of typing paper. 'Here's what we want to know – give or take a bit, because people aren't always meticulous about signing in and out. If you've popped in to do a five-minute job or to fetch something it's tempting to say to yourself, "This is bureaucracy gone mad. Who cares if I've been in or not?" And then something like this happens and everybody cares rather a lot.

'Saturday isn't the busiest time here. Families have meals or excursions to theatres or pubs. The two who left together just before Roddy did are a couple of young men who're rebuilding a scrambler motorbike. At that time there were about six people here. Two of them are making furniture – as is Roddy – and one of them uses the photographic facilities. I set that up,' Luke added with pride. 'The others don't have projects running at the moment as far as I know, so they were probably doing circuit-boards.' Angela and Violet looked puzzled. 'Perhaps I should explain that a place like this costs money to run. We have a number of very generous sponsors and the local authorities are very helpful, but power has to be paid for and materials don't always come cheap or free. So we started looking for cottage industries that could be run from here and staffed by anyone who wasn't working on a project at the time.

'We've tried a number of things from time to time. For instance, of those boys working on the boat outside, two are training as chefs and can be hired to cater for weddings and functions and there are others who can go along to wait at table. They keep a percentage of the fee plus any tips and, of course, they're setting a foot on the employment ladder at the same time. It all comes in handy for CVs.

'But one of our staunchest supporters is Jake Paterson. He has the local electronics shop, selling and servicing radios, TVs, computers, mobile phones, computers, printers, you name it. But he was a designer for a major electronics manufacturer and he's a bit of a genius, so he set up a cottage industry here making circuit boards for manufacturers. But in fact it's moved on even further, because one of his ideas for a mobile telephone answering machine looks like hitting a gap in the market and we're making most of it here. Often, there may be ten or more in that workshop, and Roddy is a regular attender. They must work very well because there are very few rejects. But they seem to enjoy it. It's very sociable. They manage to argue about almost anything from religion to politics without interrupting the work at all. Whoever's acting as foreman just has to keep them off football because it has been known for a Rangers fan to emphasize his point with a hot soldering iron.'

While he spoke he had led his two companions through the labyrinthine building. During his ownership, Sir Peter had taken advantage of every available grant to add cattle courts, milking parlours, hay and feed stores, machinery sheds and barns. Later, the benevolent builder had managed to divert a vast quantity of plasterboard which had been manufactured in a wrong size; and several weeks of work by every available volunteer under the direction of a retired clerk of works had sufficed to line every surface and to construct dividing partitions. Most of the woodwork including the cupboards under the robust benches was painted battleship grey – the one colour, Luke explained, that they could always obtain for nothing. The many apartments were only lightly occupied so comparatively early on a Sunday morning and most of the few in attendance were engaged, while donning overalls and gathering tools and materials, in bemoaning or boasting about the triumphs and disasters of the previous evening.

'This is all very interesting,' Angela said, 'but it isn't telling us where Roddy's got to.'

'That's right,' said Violet. 'Something terrible must have happened and we're standing and talking about the building.'

'Have patience. Knowledge is seldom wasted. Now we start asking questions.'

But questioning the few members present was unprofitable. It was only natural that those who had stayed late on Saturday night were to be the last in on Sunday morning and vice versa. The building was quiet and seemed very empty, but from the number of projects under plastic dustsheets on the floor or benches it would soon be buzzing like a beehive. Enquiries after Roddy Mc-William were met by only blank looks and head-shaking.

'Well, at least it seems that he didn't fall asleep over his work or electrocute himself,' Luke said. 'The two who signed out immediately after Roddy did were the manager and the treasurer. This place is very much a part-time occupation to them although they manage very well, but they're reliable Sunday attenders. We'll go back and see if they've come in yet.'

THREE

The office was no longer empty. The manager was removing a golf jacket and hanging it carefully on a wooden hanger. He looked up in surprise at the arrival of a crowd of visitors. In the small office, three was a crowd. Mr Buckley was a thin man in early middle age. His red hair was neatly cut. He had pop-eyes and an uncertain moustache. His clothes were informal but immaculate.

Luke performed introductions. It was noticeable that no mention was made of a first name for Mr Buckley. 'We're worried about Mrs McWilliam's son, Roddy,' Luke said. 'He hasn't returned home since leaving it yesterday afternoon. His intention was to come here before collecting Violet – my great-granddaughter – and going for a meal. He was duly signed in and signed out again shortly before you and Charles Hopgood left, but his mother's car is still parked in the courtyard. Did you see him?'

42

Mr Buckley seated himself on a corner of the desk. Luke, whose elderly legs were becoming tired, took the opposite corner. Mr Buckley looked amused. He met and held Luke's eyes. 'There are reasons why a young man may not go home at night – reasons that a mother may not like but needn't worry too much about. You know what I mean?' he added to Luke. His accent was carefully middle of the road but it had been cultivated on a bedrock of the Lothians.

Luke already held a dislike of the manager, on no good grounds that he could have substantiated. The suggestion of *all boys together* along with more than a hint of *nudge nudge wink wink*, especially about one who was close to Violet, was enough to put Luke's back up but he kept his temper. 'Roddy is not the sort of boy to take a dram too many and end up in the wrong bed,' he said firmly, 'and he has always been meticulous about phoning up if he couldn't keep a date with my great-granddaughter here. So did you or did you not see him?'

'We saw him,' Mr Buckley said, sobering. His voice was clipped and his sentences were terse. 'Charles and I were taking inventory ready for his audit. As you could guess it's a long business, not helped by the fact

43

that stock is changing all the time. Still, I suppose every shop has to contend with that. Much of it we may have got for little or nothing but that doesn't mean that it's free-bies for everyone. When we left, I noticed that everybody had signed out so we didn't bother to look for stragglers. There was still a Beetle in the courtyard, would that have been yours?' Angela said that it would. 'If I thought about it at all, I assumed that one of the lads who lived nearby had taken a drink and very sensibly walked home or else that one of them had left with one or two others on the razzle. Come with me.'

Luke was unable to think of a plausible excuse to remain in the office and relax in the only comfortable chair, so he got to his feet and tagged along. The building was fill-ing up. In one workshop several figures were already stooped over circuit boards. The chatter stopped but soon restarted. Mr Buckley led them back to the big joinery shop, where several separate projects were under construction and through it to a room which reeked of paint despite a venti-lation system. Somebody seemed to be try-ing his hand at French polishing. The room felt damp, which was accounted for by a bucket of water and a mop standing in a corner. The floor was almost surgically clean. Evidently dust was the great enemy.

Similar cleanliness was also evident in the photographic darkroom. Some prints were hanging up to dry; some were of sporting or landscape scenes but Luke paused to look at a shot of a pudding-faced girl with a coy smile who was shown lifting her skirt to expose frilly knickers. Luke clicked his tongue disapprovingly. Angela, encouraged by this sign, was about to express her own disapproval when Luke said, 'He knows better than that. Underexposed. No detail in the shadows at all.'

Back in the joinery shop, the large sheets of polythene serving as dustsheets were transparent and it was easy, among the larger objects, to recognize a small dinghy and a collection of furniture. Mr Buckley lifted a corner of the polythene covering some of the furniture. There were two dining chairs, a dining table and the frames for two fireside chairs. 'This is what Roddy has been working on for more than a year. He gives each piece a single coat of varnish when it's ready. When the whole collection's ready he'll finish it all together for the sake of a good match. He plans to finish it all before he marries.'

'Marries?' Violet echoed in a squeak.

Mr Buckley's pink and white face showed a smile that Luke thought contained a trace of malice. 'Did I say marries? Perhaps his words were *sets up house*. He may have been doing a little touching up last night –' the unfriendly listener might have suspected a trace of salacity in his utterance of the words *touching up* '– or he may have been putting in a little time on the circuit boards. There's a batch almost ready to go out. Come this way.'

He led them back through the woodwork shop, pointing out a bench where the almost complete frame for a settee, of similar design to the fireside chairs, was standing. 'I had no idea,' Angela said. 'He never offered to do anything like this for me. I knew he was good with his hands, but—'

Buckley glanced round but a sturdy young lady was using the planing machine at the other end of the room. There was no danger of being overheard. The smell of mahogany dust was sour in their noses. 'Did you say *good* or *free*?' he laughed.

Luke had had more than enough of Mr Buckley and to judge from their expressions so too had Violet and Angela. 'Would Mr Hopgood have seen or heard anything that you missed?' he asked.

Buckley shrugged. 'Doubt it. We were to-gether. Anyway, he's in Glasgow today.'

'What about your ... what do you call them ... members?'

'Roddy was almost the last person out other than Charles and me. I don't think any of the others could know anything.'

'He might have said something earlier to one of the others,' Violet said before Luke could suggest the same thing. 'He's very friendly with Jason Sprigg,' she added.

Buckley sighed. 'Wait in the office,' he said.

When they were alone, Violet said, 'I can't thole that man.'

Luke was in full agreement but said, 'He's a good manager. You may not like the man but have you anything tangible against him?'

Violet shook her head.

Buckley joined them in the office a minute or two later. Jason Sprigg, who followed him, was a thickset and vacant-looking boy of around seventeen. His round head seem-ed to be set on his shoulders without any neck at all. 'Now,' said Buckley, 'tell the ladies and the gentleman what Roddy said to you.'

The boy's eyebrows disappeared under his fringe. 'Everything?'

'What was the last thing that he said to you?'

' "Cheerioh." '

Buckley shrugged and turned away, his bolt shot.

'If you're setting out to be annoying, two can play at that game and I dare say I'm better at it than you are. When was this?' Luke asked. He felt a trace of compunction in letting some of his irritation with Buckley rub off on the boy, who had flushed and looked away.

'Yesterday, 'bout lunchtime.'

'Had he said anything about what he was going to do yesterday evening?' Luke asked slowly and clearly.

'Yes. He said he had a date with Vi there. Lucky sod!' Sprigg added. Violet made a small sound indicating surprise. She was only now coming to realize the power that girls have over boys.

Jason Sprigg and Mr Buckley clearly felt that they had made as much contribution to resolving the mystery as they possibly could. The three visitors were left to reconvene in the hallway.

'Shouldn't we call the police?' Violet ask-

48

ed. 'Something awful may have happened. I keep trying to think that there's an easy explanation but I don't really believe it.' Her voice was full of tears.

Angela drew breath sharply.

'It may be early for that,' said Luke. 'In fact, I don't think it's usual to treat somebody as a missing person until twenty-four hours has gone by, but that might vary from force to force and depend on circumstances. That may seem callous and unhelpful, but just imagine disappearing for an hour or two, perhaps leaving a message that didn't get to the right person, and finding the police all over you when you decided to surface. All the same, I think I might have an informal word with Ian Fellowes. He's the local detective inspector,' Luke added, in case either of his companions was unaware of it. 'Then I think we should look through the place more carefully.'

'But if Roddy signed out—' Violet began.

'I know,' Luke said reluctantly. 'Perfectly true as far as it goes. But when something as unusual as this begins you have to consider every possibility and we've no other starting point for the moment. And imagine this. Roddy says to a friend, "I must be going, I'm supposed to meet Violet in ten minutes time. I'll see you tomorrow." But he goes back into the workshops and is overcome by the fumes of paint thinners and collapses. His friend, in all innocence, signs out for him. That's just one possibility out of many. It's a very rough outline and probably miles wide of the mark, but one thing that we can do for the moment is to make sure that nothing like that happened.'

He produced his mobile phone and keyed in a number from the inbuilt directory. He compressed the mystery into about a dozen words, but a listener would have been in no doubt that he was speaking to somebody he knew well. He listened for a moment and terminated the call. 'DI Fellowes isn't too happy about it – he was planning a day in the garden – but he'll come straight down,' he said.

Luke, as a member of the management committee and the spearhead of the photographic section, was sometimes called on to officiate or to troubleshoot. Thus he was a familiar figure about the place and none of the members showed any surprise as he and his two companions explored the building, looking under benches and into cupboards, beginning with a spacious cupboard behind the office and including places where no unconscious or dead body could have arrived except by foul play. The implications were not lost on Violet, who turned progressively more blanched and shaky but soldiered on; nor on Angela, whose face became grim and tight-lipped.

They had arrived back at the entrance doors before the detective inspector's modest Vauxhall pulled up between Angela's Volkswagen and a rusty minibus. Ian Fellowes was a sturdy, sandy-haired man in his forties. No criminal had ever felt threatened by his appearance. His face was habitually calm and not unfriendly; but this apparent disadvantage (in a policeman) was frequently offset by that same criminal's dropped guard. Fellowes was a dangerous man to underestimate.

He offered them seats in his car for a discreet discussion. Angela, as the mother of the absentee, was accorded the front passenger seat. He listened patiently while the story was reiterated. 'You're absolutely certain that your search couldn't have missed anything?' he asked.

Luke nodded. 'Absolutely,' he said.

'Well, you probably know the building as well as anybody,' Fellowes said. 'I called the duty officer and set him to phoning round the hospitals. I would probably have heard by now if the boy had met with an accident. We won't start to panic yet. Just imagine how I'd look if the search parties were at work and he walked back in. And imagine the enthusiastic response I'd get, next time I needed volunteers for a search. People do turn up a substantial percentage of times, you know, and we'll hope that this is one of those times.'

Violet made a breathy sound that might have been, 'Amen'.

Fellowes glanced round the three intent faces and then went on. 'Even if the worst were to come to the worst, by which I mean Roddy failing to show up by tomorrow morning, there will be steps to be taken and if we take some of them now we will be ready to move more quickly. First, of course, somebody should be at each of your houses in case he turns up, possibly in need of help. So we'll get you home as soon as possible. And you can check your answering machines.'

'I don't have one of those gadgets,' Luke said. 'I've never had a landline phone. The Telecom wanted too much for the connection. But my house is occupied.'

'Mrs McWilliam first, then. And I'll ask

you each to prepare a list of Roddy's known friends and contacts and we'll start you phoning every single one. You never know. With a little luck he may be sleeping at one of their houses. If he's still AWOL when that's finished, we'll start getting statements from each of you.'

'We'll go straight home then,' said Luke.

Inspector Fellowes frowned for a moment in thought. 'Not yet,' he said. 'Pause for a moment outside Mrs McWilliam's house in case there's some sort of news.'

A convoy of three cars descended the hill to Birchgrove. When the town was coming into view they turned into the first group of houses. Angela's house was in the middle of the small development but the original builder had still contrived to give each house an outlook over the town to the hills beyond.

Luke and Violet were left to look over the front gardens. The high proportion of retired occupants ensured that the scene was bright with flowers. Angela, however, was not a keen gardener and her garden was tidy but green with closely mown grass. They only had a few seconds to wait before Detective Inspector Fellowes re-emerged from the McWilliam front door and beckoned. Luke moved with as much haste as he could manage but Violet was far ahead of him. She pulled up when she realized that the inspector's face was puzzled rather than pleased.

'It's Miss Grant I want rather than yourself,' Fellowes told Luke. (The two girls had accepted a change of surname to that of their great-grandfather when Luke, their nearest surviving relative, became their guardian.)

'No message?'

'There's a message, but of doubtful origin. Come and listen.'

Birchgrove had been built on a plateau detached from the main body of Newton Lauder. The cluster of small but quality houses clung to the face of a slope of rough hillside mostly covered in birch and gorse. The houses had been aimed at first-time buyers although over the years they had become occupied by widows, divorcees and one-parent families. Angela McWilliam's telephone-cum-answering machine stood on a small but highly polished table in a neat but tiny hall. The walls were hung with cheap prints of good pictures. They squeezed inside and grouped themselves around it. The inspector pressed the PLAY key.

FOUR

'Back soon, Ma,' said a voice. 'Don't worry.' The connection was broken.

The words were so few and the finish so abrupt that they were left in mid-air. The inspector broke the sudden silence. 'Again?' he suggested. The others made sounds of concurrence. The small, distorted sound was played again. 'Well?'

'That,' Angela said firmly, 'was not my son. He never, ever calls me Ma. Mama, sometimes if he's joking. More often Mum.'

'It was like his voice,' Violet said. 'It just wasn't quite right.' Her voice began to shake. 'But this means...'

Fellowes made a gesture that was intended to be calming. 'It means that there's something not quite right,' he said. 'I wouldn't put it stronger than that at the moment. I suggest that we stick to the original plan for now, except that I'll see what we can do about tracing that call.'

Luke took out and held up his mobile. 'This is the only phone I have so if he, or anyone else, tries to call me I can take it wherever I am. Perhaps I should stay here. Mrs McWilliam may need support...'

'That's kind of you, Luke,' began Angela.

'I'll stay with her,' Violet said with unusual firmness. 'You go on home, GG, in case he finds his way there.'

Angela sighed. 'You're a good girl, Violet,' she said.

'One other thing,' said Fellowes. 'Does anybody have a recording of the boy's voice so that we can make a more scientific comparison by voice prints?'

'Also on the answering machine,' said Angela. 'Roddy put on the message about the bleep and calling back. You know what I mean?'

'Of course,' said Fellowes.

Luke, feeling excluded from a largely female cabal, re-entered his car, returned to the B-road and drove home. Driving through what amounted to a tunnel beside a tumbling stream when the trees were in full leaf was one of his favourite experiences and gave real meaning to the joy of *coming home*. But this was not a day for joy. He felt his age. Jane met him at the door. 'GG, is there any news?' Her expectant look died as she saw his face.

Luke shook his head. 'Nothing here?'

'Nothing.'

Luke quitted the car and drew Jane round the house to where Helena was already seated on the terrace. The terrace was a sun-trap and life was largely lived there in fine weather. He lowered himself carefully into a garden chair and nodded to Jane to do the same. After a moment's thought he decided that Jane as well as Helena should know all that was happening. Otherwise life would soon become too complex to bear. 'Nothing at all. One answerphone message that pretended to be from Roddy. It had his accent off pat but the voice wasn't quite right. That, I'm afraid, suggests that something's wrong. I suppose it's possible that Roddy got into a mess with drink or drugs and asked somebody else to phone for him, but it's unlikely enough to be discounted. My guess would be that something's happened to Roddy and somebody else is trying to delay the start of a search. Nobody's been at the door?'

'No.' Jane turned her head away so that her great-grandfather would not see the whiteness of her face nor the tears in her

57

eyes; but Helena sensed her distress and took the young girl's hand.

Luke seldom missed any nuance of body language where his great-granddaughters were concerned. 'I was afraid so. It doesn't look good but we'll all have to be brave – and that includes you. Has Circe been walked?'

Jane shrugged. 'I took her out a little bit. I didn't want to be out of the house for too long in case there was news or Roddy even turned up here. Which he might have done if he was looking for Vi or his mum while you were all at Kempfield.'

'Quite right. Such things have been known to happen. They could happen yet.' Luke decided that the presence of a young girl during what might be a fraught period would be a distraction. 'Go and give Circe a proper walk,' he said. 'Take Violet's mobile with you, just in case.' Violet had inherited an outdated but still working mobile phone from a friend who had been given a newer model for his birthday.

Jane could quite see the advantages of being out of the house while the atmosphere was charged with anxiety and pregnant with disaster. Perhaps she might even relieve her own feelings by attempting to help, just a little bit. 'All right. Vi put the phone on charge last night in case Roddy phoned, so I can carry it switched on. You can let me know if I'm needed. Or if ... there's any news.'

She had been well trained by her great-grandfather. Although her chest felt tight and her stomach was churning, she changed her shoes and collected Violet's mobile phone. On her way through the hall she looked at the coat-stand. She seemed to remember ... Yes, there was a scarf that Roddy had left after his last visit, two days earlier. He was inclined to be careless about clothes. Given half a chance, she could cure him of that trait. She put the scarf into an unused freezer bag, whistled for Circe and set off.

Circe stuck close to heel instead of forging ahead. Jane was in no doubt that the bitch had sensed the concern that was tainting the atmosphere. She led the way into the wood and to her favourite place for thinking. The hush and the woodland smell were conducive to thought. Seated on the boulder, she told Circe, 'Be a good girl and help us.'

The bitch looked at her, head on one side, puzzled but willing.

The next step was easy. Luke had been training the two together with a view to Jane working Circe on the local shoots. An extra 'picker-up' with a good dog can be a blessing when the guns are often too busy to note the exact fall of their birds. But time can be saved if the dog knows what it is looking for. Often, a pigeon may fall during a pheasant or partridge drive. Worse, snipe or woodcock may be shot. Woodcock in particular may pose a problem by being only faintly scented. The handler may, like the dog, have been unsighted. Luke had demonstrated, using canvas dummies which had been deliberately infused with the scent of one gamebird or another, how to give the dog a taste of the scent that it should be seeking.

Jane opened the polythene bag and gave Circe a good sniff. 'Fetch Roddy,' she said distinctly. Circe gave no sign to suggest comprehension or lack of it but when Jane got up Circe turned as if for the same old walk. Jane quite understood that words, other than certain keywords, meant little to the dog but that body language, tone of voice, personal odour and perhaps even telepathy could convey messages in far more detail than the unthinking dog owner would have believed. She tried to think Roddy. The boy was fond of Circe and usually had a biscuit in his pocket for her. Jane tried to keep that picture in mind and to transmit it to the dog.

On the assumption that Roddy had not left Kempfield in a vehicle, Jane had already decided that the route giving most chance of crossing his track for the least distance covered would be to describe a circle around Kempfield. Much of it would be familiar territory. She set off towards the east and Kempfield. Circe soon fell into the most usual pattern for a gundog to follow unless told otherwise, sweeping to and fro in front of the handler. From time to time Jane refreshed the bitch's memory with a fresh sniff of the scarf. She concentrated on the dog to keep her mind off what might have happened to Roddy. Any attempt to visualize a scenario that might explain his sudden disappearance only produced visions too awful to contemplate.

They crossed a pasture where sheep, confident of the good intentions of a human figure but less certain of the dog, moved out of their path slowly at first and then as each added to its neighbour's distrust, breaking into a scamper. They gathered together in the far corner and moments later resumed cropping the grass. The trees began again. The cool, damp weather had moved on and summer had made a return. They were climbing steadily; soon Circe was panting and Jane was beginning to sweat. The midges became a nuisance but Jane was accustomed to them and had learned to ignore their fiery attack. There was running water in a ditch. Circe made for it in order to drink. Jane searched her memory and decided that there was no agricultural run-off into the ditch so the water should be safe. She bathed her face and hands before going on. She had filled her shoes with water in the process. They squelched but they were not uncomfortable.

Their way led over a crest, along the side of a field of barley stubble and through a tree strip. The buildings of Kempfield showed up beyond a field of what she thought was young oilseed rape. The distance covered was much shorter than if they had gone round by road. This was the point at which to start her circular tour. She turned north, following the hedge.

At the end of the rape-field she hesitated. Two hedges, a fence and a ditch seemed to go off in all directions with neither rhyme nor reason. She was on unfamiliar ground and for a moment she distrusted her usually reliable sense of direction. Her mind was made up for her when Circe suddenly put her nose down and forged ahead. It was an attitude that Jane recognized instantly; the dog had picked up a scent. Hoping against hope that it was not the scent of a rabbit or a pheasant, Jane followed. Circe paused, stared at the polythene bag in Jane's hand and set off again. Jane called her back and put her on the lead. It would be a bad time to be separated. Circe's pace and weight forced Jane to hurry, stumbling on the rough ground. Jane was wishing that she had put on boots rather than shoes. Her ankles needed the support.

They were following one of the hedges going slightly downhill. Soon they were back on familiar territory although she had a feeling that, in a different sense, she was venturing into the unknown. Her stomach was beginning to churn – nothing is as intimidating as the unknown danger, and adding together Roddy's absence and Circe's behaviour and tacking on the mysterious telephone message, Jane felt ready to jump at noises.

As they went along she became aware that somebody had preceded her. There was a patch of mud where an insignificant spring wetted the ground and the print of a shoe. Not a farmer's boot but a shoe. Further on, Jane recognized a set of tumbledown stone walls as what had once been a farmhouse and steading, long since left to the mercy of the weather. She had arrived there once with her great-grandfather and his lady when a farmer had intercepted them on one of their walks and asked for their help in finding a stray lamb. They had found the lamb with its fleece tangled in barbed wire but otherwise unhurt.

A cock pheasant rocketed suddenly out of a clump of gorse beside her feet, giving out its strident alarm call, and Jane only just managed to avoid biting her tongue. Sudden, explosive noise is an important part of the pheasant's escape strategy. She paused for a moment beside a large sycamore to recover her breath. The shade was welcome but the attention of the midges was not. Further on, Circe hesitated. She had crossed and ignored the trail of the pheasant, recognizing that the bird had gone away. But here was another scent, more recent than the one that she was being told to follow, and it was new to her. It was, in fact, the trail of a badger. Jane showed her the scarf again. Circe decided that Jane probably knew what she was doing. She moved forward and picked up the trail again.

GG – Luke – had warned Jane that it was a dangerous place, so she set off to skirt around the cluster of what had once been buildings but were now little more than broken walls. Circe was pulling like a tractor towards the yard between what had once been the house and the farm buildings. Jane had penetrated there with Luke in search of the lamb (which had turned up much nearer to home). But there was something very different now. She nearly missed it because of the nettles and cow parsley, but the pull of Circe took her attention. Where before there had been unbroken but hollow-sounding ground there was now a black hole the size of a chair seat, ringed with what seemed to be fragments of rotten timber. Circe followed the scent to the very brink and stood looking down.

Jane had never had a head for heights. Approaching that brink in wet socks and trainers seemed, for no good reason, more precarious that if she had arrived dry-shod. She sat and removed her wet footgear. Feeling safer in the seated position, she inched on her bottom closer to the hole, trying to avoid the nettles. Circe's tail was lashing to and fro but she looked at Jane intently. She was trying to tell the girl something.

While Jane, accompanied by Circe, was squelching her way towards the tumble-down farm buildings, Ian Fellowes was speaking to Luke on the phone. 'I've had a message relayed from North Berwick,' he said. He was in his car outside Angela's house, but he lowered his voice to save the feelings of Violet or Angela in case his words should happen to reach them. 'They've found a body. It seems to have died from a heavy blow to the head. I circulated a request to be informed of any young men found dead or injured and this is the only result so far. They want a tentative identification. Could you come with me?'

Luke was in a depressed mood and not one for looking at bodies. 'You do it,' he said.

'I don't remember ever setting eyes on the boy. I'll pick you up?'

'All right,' Luke said reluctantly. His only plan for the day had been to sit in the sun and chat to Helena, to keep his mind off Violet and the distress that she was suffering. About Roddy, he was much less concerned. 'I'm going with Ian Fellowes,' he said. 'You'll be all right? You can hold the fort and pass messages.'

'Will you be back for lunch?' she asked.

'I very much doubt it.'

Ian Fellowes decided that his own car would be slow for the journey. He phoned the police garage. When he had finished he absent-mindedly switched off his phone and dropped it into his pocket.

While the leaves were off the trees, Luke could see the roof of the police building from his bedroom window. He hardly had time to change his shoes and empty his bladder in preparation for a lengthy drive in Ian's car before Ian arrived, not in his own car but in a police Jaguar in full livery with lights and bells. 'I thought we'd be quicker in this,' he said. 'There may even be two or three more places to visit before we've finished. They wanted to give me a driver with it but the available driver's a slow-coach.'

Ian soon proved that, whatever else he might be, he was certainly not a slowcoach. He left behind a trail of taxpayer's rubber. Luke closed his eyes, clenched his fists, gritted his teeth and tried to think pure and beautiful thoughts.

FIVE

Helena was as concerned as any of the others although, as a not-quite-full-member of the family, she tried not to intrude on what she considered to be family matters until invited. She thought of herself as a guest who had never gone away. Marriage to Luke, if it ever took place, would put that to rights. This attitude usually gave her a comfortable feeling of belonging and yet being free to divorce herself from family stresses. Now, however, the inaction gave her a feeling of uselessness. The only contribution that she could think of would be to make suggestions that would probably turn out to be mere distractions. She tried to focus her attention on other tasks but on this occasion she felt unable to settle to any of the housework that she usually found therapeutic and she was staring dully at a pile of laundry awaiting ironing when Luke's mobile sounded its call. With a sense of combined relief and apprehension, she picked it up from the kitchen table and keyed it on.

'Hello?'

'Aunt Helena, is GG there?'

'That's you, is it, Jane? No. He went off with that policeman so he left his mobile with me to take any calls. There was a dead man turned up in North Berwick. We didn't see that it could possibly be Roddy but they said that they'd have to check it out. I offered to look after Vi, who I'm told is getting hysterical, but Mrs McWilliam is looking after her. She stayed there to look after Mrs McWilliam but it seems to have turned the other way around. Still, I expect it's helping each of them, having somebody to look after.' Helena sounded hurt.

'Can you reach GG?'

'I've tried twice with some not very important message about Violet but Mr Fellowes's number is always engaged. All that I get is a recorded voice telling me that the phone I'm calling—'

'Hoy!' The interruption was so unexpected, especially coming from the usually reserved and respectful Jane, that Helena fell silent. 'Aunt Helena, please, please, please stop talking and listen. This is important and urgent. I think I've found Roddy.'

'How can you not be sure?'

'I've found somebody but he's stuck down the old well at Glenshuan and I can't see who it is. I can only see the top of his head and it's too dark even to be sure of the hair colour, but who else could it be? He's alive. I can hear him making a feeble groaning sound from time to time but he doesn't answer. I've been thinking it out while I waited for someone to answer a phone. Tell GG we'll need his car and lots of rope. The coil that he has hanging in the garage would do. And he's to bring his rechargeable lamp and the torch you gave me last Christmas. And give him my old jeans off the line.'

'Have you called the ambulance? Are you hurt?'

'Aunt Helena, please listen and don't ask questions. Of course I've called for the ambulance. Now, can you remember all that I've said?'

Helena prided herself on her memory. It had never been much to write home about, but as the years passed her contemporaries' memories seemed to deteriorate so that she found herself as an elephant among goldfish. 'I think so, dear. Glenshuan. That's where we had a picnic last year while we were looking for the lamb. The well. Car.

Lots of rope. The lamp's on charge in the garage. Your head-torch. And your jeans,' she finished triumphantly.

'Well done! And he'll probably call the fire brigade, but what good they'll do I can't think. I'll leave it with you. Please, get hold of GG. He'll know what to do. He always does.'

Unaware of the compliment being paid to him by a usually unappreciative source, Luke Grant tried to relax in the passenger's seat of Ian Fellowes's police Jaguar. 'You think we're on a fool's errand, don't you?'

'I do. But what I think is of no importance. People can be seriously wrong in guessing the age of a corpse. I mean the age it was when it was alive. And this is the nearest that we've got to a lead. They'll call us if anything else turns up.' He patted the pocket that held his mobile, quite forgetting that he had switched it off. The Jaguar was so new that the radio was among the extras still to be fitted.

Helena found Angela's number in the telephone's directory and called it. Angela came on the line. 'I've just heard from Jane,' Helena said. 'She thinks she knows where

Roddy is. But I can't reach Luke or Mr Fellowes. I think the mobile's switched off.'

'Try the police station. They could reach Ian Fellowes by radio.'

Helena disliked being obliged to a woman who she could only think of as a rival, but fair was fair. 'Thank you,' she said. 'Well done.' She disconnected. She knew better than to use the emergency number for non-emergency traffic. The disappearance of Roddy McWiliam could be considered an emergency but not enough, she thought, to justify clogging up the emergency lines. She found the number for the Newton Lauder police.

A bored voice came on the line. 'Can you get a message to Detective Inspector Fellowes?' she asked.

'He's in his car.'

'I know he's in his car. That's why I can't reach him. He isn't answering his mobile.'

'Just a moment.' There was a long silence. 'His mobile isn't answering.'

'I know that.' Helena just managed not to swear. 'I just told you. Will you call him by radio? Tell him to phone Mr Grant's number.'

'Which Mr Grant?'

'He'll know. They're together.'

'If they're together why should Mr Fellowes phone him?' The voice clearly considered itself very clever.

'I didn't say that Mr Fellows was to phone Mr Grant,' Helena said through gritted teeth, speaking slowly as to an idiot. 'I said that he, or Mr Grant, must phone Mr Grant's mobile phone which I have here, in fact I'm speaking to you on it. I've some very important information about a case that they're both concerned in.'

'What case would that be?'

'It's very confidential and very important. Will you pass on the message please?'

'Very well. What was the message again?'

She managed not to scream. She disregarded a momentary fantasy involving the owner of the voice and a hot pair of curling tongs. She repeated the message and got off the line before the voice could think of any more delaying tactics. The constable, who was about to go off duty, jotted down a note for his relief.

As with any organization, the constabulary in Newton Lauder was only as good as the man who you happened to be speaking with at the time. Helena was left with no confidence that her message would ever be delivered but she took Luke's phone with her in the faint hope that she might be wrong. In the stress of the moment she was unable to think of any individual who might be able to help. It seemed to be up to her. She could at least visit Glenshuan, assess the situation and summon the fire brigade if that seemed to be the preferred solution.

A recent addition to Luke's house had been a concrete garage. It had had ivy planted around it in the hope, not so far realized, that this would help it to melt into the scenery. Luke had locked the Terios in it before his departure. He also had the key to the car in his pocket. But a spare set was kept in a kitchen drawer. After making sure that the iron was switched off, she collected the keys and the other items specified by Jane, nursed the car out on to the road and set off. Jane and Circe had trudged to Glenshuan by ways passable by a tractor but not very much else. The Terios, though a long way short of being a tractor, was a narrow vehicle with four wheel drive and a good grip on the ground. Following a now barely identifiable lane that had given access to Glenshuan when it was a working farm, she bumped along the ruts and contrived to approach right up to the tumbledown walls.

There were signs that another vehicle had been there not long before. She managed to pick a way to the former courtyard between the humps and hollows and fallen masonry.

Jane was at the driver's window immediately but her face fell. 'It's only you is it?'

'Thank you for the vote of confidence, Jane. Mr Fellowes isn't answering his mobile. I've left a message at the cop-shop that he's to phone Luke's mobile and I brought it and all the things you wanted. I thought I'd better see how things stand before calling out the fire brigade as well. Is the ambulance not there yet?'

Jane, who had now got the bit clenched between her teeth, was looking at Helena with what her adoptive mother could only think of as contempt. 'No, and anyway, what do you think any of them can do?'

'Lower somebody down...?'

'You'd better take that look.'

Helena was already out of the car. She brought out the lamp but left Luke's mobile phone on the dashboard, making sure that it was still switched on. Jane led her to the head of the well. 'Don't come too close,' she said. 'Not that you could go all the way down.'

They lay on their stomachs and shone the lamp down the hole. Jane drew in a breath through her teeth at the sight of blood. 'It's Roddy, all right,' Helena said. 'He seems to be alive – I can see his chest moving – but he's given his head a whack as he went down, or else somebody else gave him one. The stonework's rough and there's one stone about halfway down that sticks out. I think his head hit that.'

Jane made an effort to gather her wits. 'Could you imagine a grown man getting down that hole?'

Helena was beginning to wonder which was the adult and which was the child, but while Jane continued to talk unarguable sense she was not going to cavil. She judged the breadth of the shaft. 'They could dig,' she said weakly.

'It would take ages and Roddy would be dead.'

'Drop a loop...'

'Roddy went down feet first, thank goodness, but dropping loops would end up hanging him. Listen. I'm the only person around here small enough to be lowered down. I could tie the end of a rope under his arms and on to his belt. The other end would be tied to the car. You back it away and up he comes.'

To receive firm instructions from some-body of Jane's obvious youth was a new and off-putting experience for Helena, but the child was obviously still talking sense. And Helena remembered many occasions when Luke had gently coaxed Jane into applying logical rather than emotional thought to a problem. Luke, in fact, was wont to say that there were no problems, only solutions. Clearly his philosophy had found an eager pupil.

'You brought my jeans? I was imagining a whole lot of men around here and I wasn't going down head first in a skirt.'

'There aren't any men here.'

'There might be by the time you pull me up again.'

While Jane was hastily donning her jeans, Helena moved the car as close to the well-head as she could manage without risk of caving the ground in on top of Roddy. She took a more careful look. 'These stones are sharp,' she said.

Jane looked. Her mood plummeted. 'We need a pulley. Or something round. It's not going to work, is it?' she said miserably.

Helena studied her. She looked at the inert telephone. 'You're no weight,' she said.

'I could pull you up hand over hand, if you're really game to go down there.'

'I'm game.' Jane sat to tie the end of the rope to her ankles.

'Wait,' Helena said. 'That rope would damage your ankles badly.' She fetched a seat cover from the Terios and wrapped the girl's ankles before attaching the rope.

'Tie it properly,' Jane said. 'Otherwise I'll be stuck.'

'I was a scout mistress for years,' Helena said, 'long before you were born.'

'That makes me feel better. You know I'm a Guide. I'll try to keep telling you that I'm all right. If anything doesn't seem OK, haul me up quick.'

Helena knew that Jane was just babbling to cover up her nerves but she was not going to let the youngster get away with that. 'You are trying to teach your step-great-grand-mother elect to suck eggs.'

Jane smiled feebly. 'Sorry. Take the strain now.'

Helena threaded the blue rope through the towing ring of the Terios. Jane had the strap of the head-torch round her brow; she switched it on and then, quickly before she could lose her nerve, she rolled over, took the attitude of a diver and let herself slip into the mouth of the well. She was a loose fit between the rough stonework. Hanging by her ankles, she felt her insides try to slip towards her throat. 'I'm all right,' she shouted. The echo was almost stunning.

Immediately, she was lowered slowly. That was one relief. Evidently her body was not blocking off all sound. She had never suffered from claustrophobia but nevertheless she felt fear. She had checked Helena's knotwork but if the rope came away from her ankles they were in deep trouble. She would not even be able to curl round and reach her ankles to attach the rope again. A third person would have to venture down the well and she was damned if she could think of anyone small enough to go down and daft enough to do it. Already the blood was pounding in her head but she shouted again that she was all right.

The stonework was uneven and sometimes she had to make a small wriggle to slip through. She began by taking great care to avoid scraping her face against the rough and dirty stone but soon she stopped bothering. She had been disappointed that she had so far shown little sign of growing a bust, but on this occasion it was proving to be a blessing. There was no time to worry

79

whether Roddy could be pulled through the same openings. What went down could come up the same way. Parting her arms, she could see that she was descending towards the other's head. It was battered but it seemed to be seeping fresh blood from a bad graze. She thought that that meant that he was still alive.

'Stop!' she shouted. Even the person below – Roddy, she had to keep telling herself – seemed to jump at the sound.

Her descent was halted. She bobbed up and down while Helena made the rope fast to the Terios. 'Safe now,' came Helena's muffled voice.

Jane had had a better look at the unconscious man. 'It is Roddy, thank the Lord, and he's alive. Drop the other end of the rope down to me.' She was afraid that her head might burst from the pressure of the blood. Surely that never happened. But there were blood vessels ... She had several times assisted with the butchering of lambs or calves. What was trying to slip down into her chest and block her breathing would surely be classed as sweetbreads. Her mind was wandering. She got a grip and forced herself to think clearly, as GG had taught her. Roddy's arms were up towards her – as they would be after he had fallen down the shaft feet first. He would slip through a rope under his armpits. She could hear his breathing but it was faint and very laboured.

The other end of the rope came snaking down to her and stopped. She had a rough plan in her mind. 'More!' she shouted, and again, 'More!' When she thought that she had enough, she cried, 'Now make it fast.'

She made the two loops for a clove hitch and passed her left arm through them. She managed to gather both his thumbs in her left hand and she shook the double hitch down until it fell round his wrists. With that pulled tight it would probably be enough to lift him by, but *probably* was not good enough.

Roddy was not the only one struggling for breath but she drove herself on. He was wedged corner-to-corner in the shaft with slight gaps before and behind him. She dangled the spare end of rope down his front and began to curse herself for not having thought of a hook. Helena could cut a twig or a bramble but that would take time and time was running out. If she went back up to recover she would never muster the resolve to come down again. She reached down Roddy's back but her arms were not long enough.

'Lower me a few more inches,' she called out. She felt herself creep downward. There was still not enough space. The human body is wonderfully adaptable. It flexes. It compresses. Jane's and Roddy's bodies were doing both as she fought to get a grip on the rope. She forced herself onward and downward, stretching an inch at a time, jamming her head and shoulders down behind his shoulder blades, forcing her hand round past male bits and pieces. With her other hand she twiddled the rope until, miraculously, her fingertips touched something that swung away and which was not a part of Roddy McWilliam. She tried again, hooked a finger round it and drew in the spare end of rope. Somebody had hinted that harm could come to a young man in such ways, but survival took precedence. She pulled the rope up tight between his legs and passed it through his belt. At her call, Helena pulled her up for a few feet. Hastily, because her strength was already at an end, Jane knotted the end to the hitched rope at his wrists.

'Pull me up,' she shouted. There was a delay while Helena straddled the wellhead and took a firm hold on the rope. Soon Jane

82

was moving, slowly and jerkily, but definite- ly upwards. She was able to help by pushing with her hands against the bumps and hol- lows in the shaft of the well. When she look- ed up for the first time between her knees, it was Circe's brown eyes that she saw looking down anxiously at her.

Luke and the detective inspector were on the way home. Much of the return journey had been taken up by a running diatribe concerning the officer who had reported the corpse. 'You would think,' said Fellowes, summing up, 'that the silly beggar could have mentioned that the body was two metres tall, had an artificial leg and had obviously been in the water for a week at the very least. Oh well!' He handed over his mobile phone. 'We'd have heard if there was any news, but you may as well give the Newton Lauder nick a ring for me.'

Luke took the phone. He looked and look- ed again. 'It's not switched on,' he said.

Ian Fellowes choked back an expression that serving officers are not supposed to know, let alone use. He swerved on to the hard shoulder, pulled up and took back his phone.

'Messages?' Luke said.

'There are indeed messages.' The first was a garbled version of the message that Helena had left for him. The number of Luke's mobile was already recorded in his phone. He keyed it up and called it.

Jane rolled at last out of the wellhead and on to firm ground. She lay limp. 'I'm beat,' she said.

Helena said nothing. She was too busy with breathing heavily and trying to ignore the pain in her arms and shoulders.

'I'm totally pooped,' said Jane. 'I'm shattered. But we'll have to finish the job and get Roddy out of there.' She sat up and began to untie her ankles. 'At least there are two of us now.'

'But he's heavier than you are.'

'Not by much. I've been teasing him about being so skinny.'

'We'll do it quick before exhaustion takes over.'

The two faced each other across the wellhead and took it in turns to haul. The rope came taut but Jane's knotwork held. If either of them thought that the other was doing less than her share she had more sense than to say so. Whenever Roddy stuck, the trick was to lower him and try again. Roddy was halfway up when Luke's phone called for attention. A previous owner, a joker, had caused the original tune to be replaced by a female voice calling, in insinuating tones, 'I'm ready!' Luke had retained the adaptation. It made a useful conversation piece.

The voice failed to register with Jane or Helena for several seconds. Then Helena said, 'Take a break,' and backed away, picking up the phone as she went and dragging the rope under a rear wheel to anchor it. Jane lay back and gave way to exhaustion.

The detective inspector's questions were brusquely cut off by Helena. 'Can't talk now. We're rescuing the boy. Come quick. We're still waiting for an ambulance.'

'Where are you?'

'We're at...' Helena's memory failed her. 'Where are we?' she asked Jane.

'Glenshuan.'

Helena repeated the name and switched off. 'Come here,' she called.

Jane dragged herself to her feet and moved to Helena's side with dragging footsteps. The delay had given time for the midges to follow the smell of their sweat and turn their lives to misery. Together they managed to disengage the rope from under the wheel and resume the agony of hauling. At last his arms and then his head emerged. Between them they managed to work out a way of extracting him without letting him slip. They lifted him out carefully and laid him down gently, turning his head so that the damage was uppermost and pillowing it on Jane's discarded skirt, folded small.

'Good Lord!' Helena exclaimed. 'He is in a mess.'

'Not as bad as he looks. I was sick all over his head and some of that blood's from my nosebleed.'

'Oh. That's a relief. I thought it was the other way round, that the blood on your face had come from him. I don't think that your injuries are very urgent, but he's breathing very badly. One of us had better give him mouth-to-mouth. The kiss of life,' she added.

At one time Jane had dreamed of touching lips with Roddy, but now that she was a little older and becoming more aware of the significance of kissing the very idea over- whelmed her. She kept her head down, un- tying her knots. 'You'd better do it.'

'My dear, the way I'm puffing I'd probably burst his lungs.' Helena wanted nothing in the world more than to rest her back. She was already lying prone while rubbing her ears to try to relieve the agony of the midge-bites. 'You know how?'

'We had lessons. But I was sick while I was hanging upside down.'

'I don't think he'll mind terribly much.'

So Jane, after spitting violently many times to get rid of the taste of her sickness, found herself lip to lip with her idol. Helena rolled her knees from side to side, her usual method of relieving back pain. Jane kept Roddy breathing. Whenever she took a rest his lungs faltered again. The combined pain and delight seemed to last forever.

Relief arrived at last on foot in the form of GG and Ian Fellowes. They were leading two burdened paramedics, who they had found in their ambulance, searching without much hope for Glenshuan under the impression that it was still a working farm.

The arrivals took in the scene. The paramedics opened their stretcher beside Roddy but conferred urgently by radio with somebody at their base before moving him. Luke's instinct, honed by sixty years as a professional, impelled him to use the miniature digital camera that lived always in his breast pocket. Then his concentration transferred from Roddy to Jane. 'My God! What happened to you? You're all over blood.'

Jane began to straighten. 'It's mostly Roddy's. What's mine comes from my nosebleed.'

'Don't stop breathing for him,' one of the paramedics said urgently. Jane resumed her task but taking care to keep her still bare feet out of the way of their boots.

'But I want to know about my great-granddaughter,' Luke complained.

Helena was feeling better. 'I could take over now,' she offered.

'It's all right.' The other paramedic produced a mask and a very small oxygen cylinder. 'This will last him as far as the ambulance.'

'That's good,' Jane said. She sat back on the ground. Her magical moment was over. She had time at last to look around. The view from where they were between the ruined buildings took in a panorama of woods and fields in their full glory. She had seen them before but never had they looked so good. Circe, who had been made anxious by the strange goings-on and had had to be restrained from trying to lick off the blood, tried to crawl into her lap. Jane put her arms around the dog and the two sat huddled together. 'I was running out of puff. He *is* going to make it?' Jane asked anxiously.

The two paramedics exchanged a glance. The older of the two said, 'I doubt if anybody could tell you that for sure yet. What I can tell you is that you weren't a moment too soon.'

'What nosebleed?' Luke was demanding. 'What happened to you?'

'From hanging upside down. And I'd better tell you that that's my sick all over him, not his.'

'That's a relief,' said one of the paramedics. They finished fastening a neckbrace and lifted Roddy very gently on to their stretcher. One of them was looking hopefully at the Terios. The other shook his head. 'We can give him a smoother ride carrying. It's not very far.'

'You're all right, then?' Luke asked Jane.

'You'd better phone Mrs McWilliam and let her know that Roddy's alive. I'm fine, except that I'm hungry. We've missed lunch and I seem to have sicked up my breakfast.'

'She'll be all right,' said one of the paramedics, laughing.

SIX

The first task, even before re-entering the Terios, was performed by Luke after he had recovered his mobile. This was to follow Jane's suggestion that he should let Angela and Violet know that Roddy had been rescued and was on his way to the local hospital for first repairs. He would be taken from there to the New Edinburgh Royal Infirmary (the 'New Royal').

Luke, Helena and Jane then adjourned home. Jane had bathed, repaired her many cuts and scratches with sticking plasters and changed into clean, dry clothes. She was, she said, feeling less like something that a starving warthog had nibbled and rejected. They were satisfying their immediate hunger-pangs with microwaved snacks from the freezer when Violet and Angela arrived, fresh from the hospital and very shaken. They had been allowed to look at Roddy through a window. Roddy had been cleaned of blood and sickness but he remained white and limp between the bandages and when Angela, as his mother, had demanded a prognosis she was met with evasive answers. The mood of the group was therefore a blend of celebration that he had been found and recovered alive and a greater anxiety as to whether he would stay that way. Each individual strove to adhere to the optimistic line so that a superficially cheerful party developed with only occasional silences. Their efforts were enhanced by Luke's production of a two-litre box of claret and by a magnum of Champagne that Angela had been saving for a special occasion. She could not think of a better use for it than to toast Roddy's chances of a full recovery. Even the teetotal Circe had a festive air. She might not understand fully what she had helped to achieve but there could be no doubt that the whole gathering was pleased and that she was in very good odour. She frisked and made the most of the edible rewards that came her way.

Policemen and firemen are usually too busy to make phone calls during an emergency and it is left to the ambulance men, who may be standing by for long periods at a time, to maintain relationships with news editors and to pocket welcome backhanders for the occasional tip-off. Luke's profession as a photographer had made his phone number well known to the press and so, despite the day being Sunday, it was not surprising that his mobile began to demand attention. Luke performed the electronic equivalent of hanging up on the first few reporters to phone, but Newton Lauder is not so very far from Edinburgh. Two cars brought three reporters and a photographer. There was a brief dispute while each reporter tried for an 'exclusive' and while Jane, aided by Luke, negotiated payment for a story that was generally agreed to be hers to tell. The story, and the fee, was shared between two papers. The reporters consumed a share of the Champagne but, in a gesture of fairness and to keep the party going, one of them went down into Newton Lauder for another box of claret.

Luke's sitting room was decorated in pale grey but the walls were hardly seen behind the ranks of framed photographs that provided the colour. The room, which usually seemed quite spacious, was beginning to seem overcrowded. Tongues were loosened. Violet became tearful and was put to bed. Jane was not old enough to drink but blind eyes were turned and she was allowed a little wine, well watered whether she knew it or not. Jane, while attempting to behave with modesty, was led on by the others. Coming down from her high, her moods were swinging around the compass.

Luke phoned the hospital three times and each time the news was a trifle less foreboding. Roddy was not only surviving but had regained enough strength to be moved to Edinburgh. Jane, the paramedics and the doctors each felt responsible for the improving prognosis.

Angela who, in her relief, was tippling along with the rest, was becoming tearful. Reporters develop a knack of asking questions which, though apparently mindless and free from guile, may be calculated to provoke the witness into unguarded disclosures. Helena had already told at some length the story of Jane's trip down the well and her own agonies of fear in abetting the dangerous adventure. Angela was asked how she felt about Jane's courage in being lowered head first into the unknown. She left nobody in any doubt that she felt very strongly indeed. It soon became clear that she was becoming confused between Jane and Jane's elder sister. From being sweethearts she had the young couple engaged and then married and by the time that Ian Fellowes arrived she was doting on her grandchildren, the first of which would be called Jane, whether a girl or, apparently, a boy.

Without losing the amiability of his expression, the detective inspector got rid of the reporters. Luke followed them outside. They had the story in words, though they had been allowed to believe that Roddy's descent into the well had been the merest accident. However, their photographs of Jane and Circe, the heroines of the day, rather lacked immediacy and impact. Luke, without grudging Jane the glory of the moment or the rewards that came with it, saw no reason why she should be the only person to profit. He was able to show, on the camera's own little monitor, several shots of Roddy, prone and bloodied beside the wellhead, with Jane in a not dissimilar state administering the kiss of life, Circe watching approvingly, Helena exhausted and then the newly arrived paramedics beginning to attend the injured. A valuable little auction ensued on the spot.

Ian Fellowes's news was lower key. His first step towards finding out what had brought Roddy from Kempfield to near the bottom of a well at Glenshuan Farm, nearly two miles away, had been to question those known to have been at Kempfield around the time of Roddy's visit. But he had been unable to make contact with the manager or the treasurer at Kempfield. Mr Buckley lived alone and there was no answer at his door or from his telephone. Charles Hopgood was sometimes referred to as the cashier and sometimes as treasurer but his role was considerably more senior, being more akin to financial director. He was often referred to as 'Doctor' Hopgood. The only doctors of that name figuring in the Medical Register were easily accounted for, so it was presumed, by Luke and others, that his doctorate was in one of the many subjects that are grouped under the general heading of Philosophy. He had a wife but no one had been able to get hold of her either.

Of the two young men who had left Kempfield just ahead of Roddy, one had been contacted. He rather thought that he had seen Roddy in the background just before leaving the building but had no recollection as to what he had been doing. The other seemed to have disappeared as cleanly as had Roddy earlier, but he had been boasting about his hot date for the evening so his friends and family were a long way from becoming worried. It was not the first time and it would not be the last.

'Off the top of the head,' Ian said, 'I see very little worth doing at this hour of a Sunday night. Our missing person has turned up. We now have missing witnesses instead. We know that something's wrong but we don't know what, which rather limits the useful questions to be asked. It is now becoming rather late on a Sunday and I'm not supposed to be on duty at all. I shall leave it until morning and then start an enquiry going, assuming that by then I have a better idea of what I want to know. And just in case Dr Hopgood and Mr Buckley have taken Roddy's place in the ranks of the missing, would you, Mr Grant, please see if you have any useful photographs of them among your back numbers?'

Luke said that he would.

'Surely,' Jane said, 'Roddy will tell you all you need to know when he comes round.'

Inspector Fellowes smiled on her. He refrained from pointing out that Roddy might not come round at all. 'I would like to think so,' he said. 'But when somebody has hit their head or had a knock on it, the brain can be bruised. There's nearly always some loss of memory, usually of events just before the knock on the head. Sometimes that part of the memory returns quickly, sometimes it takes longer and sometimes it never returns at all.'

'I should have thought of that for myself,' Jane said. 'My mum was like that before she died, wasn't she?'

Ian Fellowes nodded. 'So unless Roddy comes round and tells us that he fell down the well by accident, like Pussy—'

Jane was still above herself. Moreover, she was the only person present young enough to be familiar with nursery rhymes. 'Pussy didn't fall down the well by accident,' she said. 'She was pushed in by Little Johnny Thin.'

'I suspect,' said the DI, 'that Little Johnny Thin has a perfect alibi. But we'll have to accept that there may have been some dirty work taking place. With no witnesses or other evidence yet, we have to assume that he was attacked. He may have been thrown down the well, or pushed, although in either eventuality you would not have expected him to go down feet first. To judge from the fragments of rotten wood caught up in his clothing it looks as though the boards covering the well gave way under his weight. According to the doctors, he was struck a violent but glancing blow such as would probably be the case in an accidental fall down the well. He received several other blows to the skull, one a direct, almost square-on blow and another a glancing blow, but neither was heavy enough to damage the skull and it looks as though he fell, bumping his head and limbs on the way down, and then hit it a damaging blow near where he came to rest. The shaft of the well is rough but it has only one seriously protruding stone that he could have landed on.'

Luke had developed a hard head over the years and though he was feeling mildly elevated he was still following the arguments. 'At first glance,' he said, 'it doesn't look like a serious assault but more like an accident. The footprints around the well didn't tell you anything?'

'Nothing,' Fellowes confirmed. 'Two ladies hauling a load that was really too heavy for them up a forty-foot shaft were staggering about and beating the weeds down. Then everybody else milled around and completed the eradication of every meaningful track. However, we have no explanation for how he came to leave Kempfield on foot and, according to one witness, by the back door. He then headed cross-country in the general direction of this house and ended up near the bottom of a well that is a long way off the shortest route. So it seems likely that I shall be asking each of you for a statement and it would help and save time if you made a start on drafting it tonight or first thing in the morning.'

The inspector then took himself off, leaving his witnesses, as he thought, to start drafting their statements. Those witnesses, however, were only too well aware of being mildly inebriated, tired and, by turns, either worried or exuberant. It was generally agreed that the morning would be quite soon enough. Mrs McWilliam, exhausted by an excess of worrying, had already fallen asleep. She proved to be too unhandy a burden to be carried upstairs even with so many willing pairs of hands available, so she was bedded down on the settee in the sitting room and covered with the quilt from the spare bedroom.

The next day was the Monday which, properly speaking, should have been a school day; but even before they went to bed on the Sunday night it was agreed that Jane would be kept off school. Luke surmised that there would be enough publicity to destroy any chance of a day at school being a learning occasion. He also guessed, rightly, that she and Helena would both be suffering from the muscular strain and the letdown after the adrenaline rush. Each was allowed to lie in until ready to face the world and the physical effort of getting dressed.

Violet's case was slightly different. She was serving an apprenticeship with a local architect. She had suffered no physical strain. The news was that Roddy, who had had a peaceful night, was suffering from some skull damage but was strong enough to bear surgery to it. Luke decided that Violet, despite any emotional storm that she might have suffered, was quite fit enough to go to her work and to be a serious nuisance if she didn't. She was packed off in time to catch her usual lift.

There was little need for the explanations that Luke offered to Violet's employer and Jane's headmaster. The Scottish media that morning were dominated by a highly glamorized version of the story of the young girl who, aided by a dog that she had trained, found a missing boy and then, before professional help arrived, was lowered head first down the well by her stepmother in order to rescue him. Even the Nationals and the TV news channels repeated the story, avoiding with their usual hypocrisy any mention of the dog having been trained for the gun. But that was not the end of it. Dogs and young girls are newsworthy and photogenic. A visit from a TV journalist with cameraman resulted in a news item that was widely repeated and which led in turn to invitations for Jane to appear on several of those TV shows that lurk on the borderline between news and chat. But that was for later. For now, it is enough to say that Jane, carefully briefed by her great-grandfather, performed with creditable modesty, relayed an appeal for information composed for her by Detective Inspector Fellowes and enjoyed the whole experience enormously.

One of the advantages that Luke found in depending entirely on a mobile phone was that he did not appear in any directories. Anybody having his mobile number had it because he had wished them to have it. Unfortunately, thanks to his work as a photographer, most of the media had had his number pressed on them, but few were so efficient as to connect the elderly Luke Grant, great-grandfather of the heroine of the day, with L. Grant, Photographer. Thus there were some precious intervals between calls from media-persons wanting telephone interviews or appointments for photo sessions.

During one of those precious intervals DI Fellowes arrived, accompanied by a frumpish woman constable, both in plain clothes. The middle of the working day was spent by Luke and Jane and Helena in turn in the sitting room, producing their draft statements and refining them under questioning by Ian Fellowes while the woman constable recorded them in shorthand as well as on tape. Whoever was taking a turn at answering the telephone simply carried it with them and, when appropriate, read out a prepared statement. For the most part, Luke kept Jane close to him, watching her carefully in case of any reaction from the previous day's excitements. The reaction that he most feared was a swelled head.

One thing that Luke had noticed during his lifetime of dealing with the media as a freelance photographer was that when the mediocrities (as he had begun referring to the ladies and gentlemen of the media) were starved of detail they would certainly invent it and if cameras were evaded there would soon be a state of siege. A press conference was hastily arranged for the evening of the following day and was included in the prepared statement. It was to take place in the Newton Lauder Hotel, where the manager, always alert for sources of extra business, had placed the function room at their disposal.

Ian Fellowes had prepared another list of questions that he wanted put to the public. From one of these it was clear that the police would very much like to speak with Mr Timothy Buckley (manager of the Kempfield Centre), Dr Charles Hopgood (the treasurer and financial director) and Mrs Hopgood. When the detective inspector revealed this particular desire, which he did as hesitantly as if he had been admitting to a fancy for young boys, Luke's eyebrows went up. 'They have all disappeared? All of them?'

'Let's just say that we have so far been unable to question any of them. No neighbours seem to have set eyes on any of them since yesterday evening.' He looked from Luke to Helena and Jane, and shrugged. 'Don't quote me, because so far as we know none of them has misbehaved in any way, but three more sudden disappearances do suggest that something's amiss. And surely there can't be another three forgotten wells to explore.' He glanced at Circe, sprawled on the hearthrug, as if wondering whether to send her on a search of abandoned farms. 'The possibilities are almost infinite, when you consider that any one or two or even all three of them may be quite innocently away, or in hospital, in quarantine, dead or injured, restrained under duress, in flight for fear of reprisals or of becoming incriminated in something, and probably half a dozen other explanations for absence that I haven't thought of yet. A message on the lines I've suggested will surely turn up something of interest.'

'That,' Luke said, 'might depend on what interests you.' If Jane had not been present he might have gone on to suggest that the three might be indulging in a threesome orgy at some disreputable club or hotel. 'You do realize that you'll be telling the world's media that this isn't about a boy who fell down a well by accident. You'll be broadcasting the fact that there were shenanigans at Kempfield and, by implication, that Roddy McWilliam was involved, one way or the other.'

'Almost certainly as an innocent victim.

Be that as it may,' the DI said, 'any request for information coming from here just now will set them thinking. What must be must be but we'll try not to let any bad publicity attach to the Kempfield Centre. My job has become measurably easier since Kempfield opened so its continued success is very precious to me. I've had little or no contact with any of the three. You, on the other hand, as a committee member at Kempfield, must have had some contact, at least with the men.'

'On a business rather than a social level,' Luke said.

If Ian Fellowes's relaxed air suggested somnolence, that impression was immediately corrected. 'Which of them did you dislike?' he asked sharply.

'I beg your pardon?'

'Your voice expressed distaste. Tell me all that you can about any of the three. And don't pull any punches. What I need is the truth.'

'Very well.' Luke paused to gather the thoughts that had never before been called to the forefront of his mind. 'Away from Kempfield, they hardly mix with other townsfolk. I don't know the lady, Mrs Hopgood, at all,' he said at last. 'She's early middle-aged, just leaving youth behind, plump, blonde – I wouldn't know real from bottle, you'd have to ask another woman about that. I think that she has a roving eye and a flirtatious manner but I don't know why I think that. It's probably just from seeing her posture from a distance and noticing how men's body language changes when she's mentioned. I've never even heard her voice or seen her close to.

'Her husband is a big man with a loud voice and the better sort of Edinburgh accent. His high colour probably makes him seem even larger than he really is. He's sometimes addressed as 'Doctor' but I've no idea of what. He seems to be a good treasurer and financial director, thrifty with Kempfield's money, but I can never make head nor tail of his reports and balance sheets. I seem to remember that he proposed Buckley for manager, so there may be some sort of relationship there. I think that they have some sort of business interest in common, but it isn't local to here so I know nothing about it. They each live in Newton Lauder. The Hopgoods have one of those rather secluded houses on the Edinburgh Road. I don't know where Buckley lives.'

'I think he has one of those flats in Airglen

Close,' Jane said. 'The ones that are always changing hands because the rooms are so small. I've seen him there more than once when I've been visiting *my friend* Marie Campbell.'

'Thank you, Jane. He's younger and smaller than Hopgood, with red hair and slightly bulging eyes. He seems to have started growing a moustache and then given up the effort. I don't know what else I can tell you. Their CVs should be on file somewhere in Kempfield. I must have seen those at one time but I've no recollection of their past histories.'

'Would you have photographs of the three?' the DI asked.

Luke frowned. 'Probably. I'll have Violet take a look when she gets home. She's taken over most of my processing and all my filing and she's very good at it. After all, I was already a father and within a cough and a spit of being a grandfather when computers came into common use. I have learned to use them after a fashion, just as one might learn to use a camera without knowing how or why it works, but she is of the generation that grew up with them. Off the top of the head, I don't remember any shots of Buckley or the Hopgoods but there must have been many taken at dances, garden parties, all sorts of formal events where there were too many people present to be indexed as individuals. Those three may have been avoiding the public eye, but we had a party in the big workshop at Kempfield when the last extension was finished and the manager and the treasurer could surely not have avoided that. I'll have Violet see what we can find and if there's anything to be found we'll run off some copies to be distributed. I'll ask her employer to let her get away early.'

'Splendid,' Ian Fellowes said. He looked doubtfully at Jane. 'I think that we could enjoy a cup of coffee.'

Luke took the hint. 'Jane, would you mind?'

Jane was aware that she was being shunted into a siding, but she trusted her great-grandfather to tell her whatever she might have missed. When the door closed behind her, Ian Fellowes said, 'This is definitely not for publication just yet, but we caught up with the boy who spoke to Roddy last. His name's Hamish Todd. His story – and he tells it convincingly – is that he was tidying away some materials in the circuitboard workshop when Roddy came in. I understand that there are fire escape doors in there?'

'That's right.'

'Roddy came in and made for those doors. He was pushing against the panic bolts, appropriately enough, because Todd says that he was showing signs of panic. While he was struggling—'

'Those bolts are very stiff,' Luke confirmed. 'Perhaps dangerously so.'

Fellowes nodded. 'Anyway, Todd asked him what was up. Roddy said, "I heard them talking. There's going to be hell to pay. And they realized—" At that moment the bolt shifted and the door opened and Roddy almost fell out and took to his heels. One of the men followed – he can't remember which – and closed the outside door. Todd was left wondering what it was all about, but he was much more interested in his prospects with his date for the evening. He checked that the fire escape door was properly closed and put it out of his mind. It's a reasonable working assumption that they followed him up.'

'And put him down the well feet first and still breathing. That seems a remarkably undecided way to go about it. I mean, if somebody's happened on your guilty secret you either knock them off or you don't. You might, I suppose, assault them as a warning to lay off and to keep your mouth shut. What you wouldn't do is to leave them alive in circumstances that would make any rescuer wonder what was going on and ask a lot of questions that the victim would by then be only too eager to answer.'

'I see what you mean,' said Ian Fellowes. He lowered his voice further. 'There's one other thing, and this is top secret even from your great-granddaughter for now. I sent a small team into Kempfield this morning to see what signs and portents they could pick up. There were signs that the lock on the front door had been forced.'

That certainly made Luke sit up. He had been aware that, from a beginning in which the building had no contents other than material that had been scrounged or obtained at a mighty discount, it had come to contain some valuable machinery, the expensive components for the circuit boards and some quality items fabricated by the members. There were two rifles under reconstruction in respect of which he was unsure of the legal status. 'The members all know the combination of the entrance lock,' he pointed out.

'I do know that,' Fellowes snapped. 'I advised you about that when the question of security was discussed. But that isn't the end of the matter. There is what seemed to be a locked cupboard at the back of the office.'

'It was built as a filing room but never used. The files are all on computer now.'

'It has been used all right,' the DI said grimly. 'There's a plastic-topped table in there, a box of small medicine bottles, some blank lables and traces of white powder that have gone for analysis.'

Luke slumped in his chair. 'Oh God!' he said. 'Oh holy hell! I thought that that was one danger that we'd steered clear of so far. There was an outbreak of pot smoking at one time and the culprits were banned for several months and given a sterner warning than you could have got away with. That seemed to spread the word that drugs were not acceptable at Kempfield. What they get up to at home is their parents' business. And yours, of course.'

Ian Fellowes nodded with sympathy. 'If those traces turn out to be what I suspect, your young members can't be to blame. That little secret room would only be regularly accessible to staff.'

'We're staffed almost entirely by volunteers.'

Jane came back with coffee and the subject was dropped for the moment.

SEVEN

An arrangement that suits everybody would be rare indeed. For the media conference, Luke had decided to select a time that at least suited *him* and had defended his decision against all arguments. The media conference had been called for eight p.m., which was, inevitably, too late for whatever deadline had most recently passed and left too little time before the one rapidly approaching or too much time for the news to remain fresh or exclusive. Despite their loud complaints, a substantial number of persons qualifying, however loosely, as reporters, correspondents, cameramen, sound men and numerous other specialists began to drift into the function room (principally from one or other of the hotel's bars) before seven, each hoping for first choice of the best strategic position.

Ian Fellowes had contrived to borrow four large constables, under his own control and that of Luke (whose experience of such events stretched back more than half a century). Between them they managed to prepare a sensible arrangement of seating and to prevent war breaking out over the best camera positions and occasional attempts to position light-reflecting umbrellas where they would prevent a rival's cameras from seeing anything whatever. Luke was feeling uneasy. Photographers are not judged on their outward image and ever since he had missed a stunning news shot because care for his one good suit had kept him back from the action Luke had lived and worked in clothes that already showed signs of a hard life. Tonight, however, Helena had forced him into his newest and least disreputable suit and he felt inhibited.

When the representatives of radio, TV and the press were more or less settled, some members of the public were admitted, habitual hecklers and those already under the influence being ruthlessly excluded. The room was only sparsely occupied at first although it was filled with murmuring and the smell of whisky.

As the locals took note of the TV vans and other signs the room began to fill up. Unlike the Town Hall it boasted no sporting memorabilia but was boldly decorated in contemporary fashion without any trophies to agitate the softhearted. Rather than risk interruption of the proceedings or missing of a vital phone call, Luke left his mobile with one of the constables guarding the door. Calm fell just after eight twenty, which by local custom was remarkably prompt, and the proceedings were called to order by Ian Fellowes. The fame of Kempfield was becoming almost widespread but Ian, responding to a plea and a careful briefing from Luke, slipped in a summary of Kempfield and its objectives in the guise of background. The participants, he said, would each tell their parts of the story in chronological order and, when all had had their say, time would be allowed for questions.

Angela McWilliam was the first speaker. She must have had some experience of such affairs because when the first TV lights blazed on her she remained unworried but produced a pair of dark sunglasses and put them on. Her voice held a slight tremor as she described her worry when her son failed to come home, two nights earlier. Neither he nor his girlfriend was of the irresponsible type.

It was soon Jane's turn. Luke had advised her how to comport herself; in particular to speak clearly, take her time and be sure to say exactly what she meant. She started well. While her sister, her great-grandfather, Mrs McWilliam and DI Fellowes had searched the buildings at Kempfield and then become busy with other lines of enquiry, she had felt useless. Like a spare prick at a wedding, she added.

There was an immediate but subdued babble of mingled shock and laughter. Luke spoke quickly to Jane. 'That's not an expression you should ever use,' he said. And to the ladies and gentlemen of the media, 'Please edit that out.' Most of them did so, but the clip surfaced occasionally in TV compilations of the most shocking moments genre.

Jane was scarlet. 'Well, I didn't know that it was rude,' she said. 'It's just something I heard somebody say once.'

Luke knew better than to labour the point. He made a mental note to find out later who had spoken so incautiously in the presence of his great-granddaughter. 'Calm down and go on,' he told Jane.

Jane did as she was bid, but in a voice so quiet that she was several times asked to speak up. 'I thought that there was one way I might at least try to be useful and it would get me out of everyone's way. I had spent a lot of time training Circe, our young Labrador, to follow a scent.'

'She's *your* young Labrador,' said Luke.

'Well yes. But I didn't like to say that. I was afraid that it might sound like boasting. She isn't exactly a bloodhound, but GG – my great-granddad – says she's got a very good nose. Roddy had left his scarf behind, last time he was in our house, and I held it for her to sniff. The only place we knew for sure that he'd been was at Kempfield so I thought that if we started by making a circle around the Kempfield buildings we might find a trail. If that failed, it would have to be zigzagging around and hoping for the best. Of course, Roddy could have left Kempfield in someone's car or even by bicycle, but at least I couldn't have done any harm and I'd have been out of everybody's way.

'Near Kempfield, Circe seemed to have found a scent. Of course, there was no way I could be sure that it was Roddy she was scenting and not a rabbit on ... or something.' Luke had impressed on her not to mention pheasants or foxes. 'But I kept on showing her the scarf and –' Jane smiled suddenly, her shyness overcome '– do you know, I'm sure she was nodding at me impatiently, just the way my great-granddad does.' There was a ripple of laughter. 'Anyway, she led me to Glenshuan, where there'd been a farm at some time but it's been abandoned for yonks. Years, I should say. The buildings are falling down, people have been pinching the stones for newer buildings and in places there's not much more than foundations left, mostly the rubbish stones that nobody wants to pinch for building. I mean, any old stone will do where you can't see it.

'There's a courtyard in the middle and in the middle of that there's an old well. There had been heavy boards over it but they'd become rotten over the years and they were falling away. Something had broken through and that's where Circe led me.'

Jane paused for breath and looked at her great-grandfather. He nodded.

'It was rather a scary place but I crawled to the edge and looked down. The ... the shaft or whatever you call it is quite narrow. In fact, it's so narrow that I wonder how they managed to build it, because there's nothing like enough room for a mason to go down the middle of it, but GG says that there are tricks for doing that sort of job. Anyway, there was very little light – my head seemed to blot out most of it – but I thought I could see somebody's head and when I listened very carefully I was sure that I could hear breathing, faint and not very regular but breathing all the same. Of course, when things are creepy you often think you hear breathing, but this time I was sure.' There was a rustle of not unsympathetic amusement.

'We have a spare mobile phone and I'd brought that along. I tried to phone GG – my great-granddad – but he was with Mr Fellowes and that phone wasn't answering and while I waited I thought it out. I didn't want to wait for the ambulance or fire brigade, because the ... the shaft of the well was so small. I was probably the only person around who could get down there. Roddy's quite slim and he seemed to have slipped down as far as a slim person could go. My sister has a bigger – I mean, she's sort of wide across the ... the hips,' Jane said carefully. The laughter was renewed, a little louder this time. 'And I was quite sure there wasn't time to dig. So I phoned home and spoke to Aunt Helena.' She pushed her chair back thankfully out of the glare of the TV lights. She was perspiring gently from their heat.

At Ian's nod, it was Helena's turn. She had at first shown signs of terror at the prospect of speaking in public and being recorded for even more public attention, but a reporter who had often bought Luke's photographs to illustrate his scoops had taken her into the bar and fed her several brandies. The dosage had been nicely judged. Helena spoke up with unusual confidence and her speech was only slightly slurred. 'You won't want a recital of everything that passed through my mind. I thought I'd better take a look before doing anything too dramatic. I didn't know what was in Jane's mind and I'd probably have chickened out if I had, but she had seemed quite calm and logical so I did as she suggested and brought the coil of rope from the garage and I took Mr Grant's four-by-four.

'I knew where Glenshuan is. When I got there, which was far from easy because the old farm tracks aren't used much any more and they're overgrown and rutted, I could see that Jane was absolutely right. We could have phoned around all night but unless the fire brigade or the potholers or somebody had a midget among them we wouldn't find anyone more suitable than Jane and she was keeping her head amazingly well. I wouldn't have gone down there myself even if I could, not for all the tea in China, but she'd made up her mind and being a Guide she knows about knots and things. As she'd pointed out very sensibly, dangling a loop would only have resulted in hanging him.

'There would be no turning around down there, of course, so she'd have to go down headfirst with her arms extended, but she insisted that she was game. I had my doubts but I was sure that I could always pull her up again. I did think about phoning around for one or two men to do the pulling up, but I decided that time was probably of the essence and that I was strong enough to lift Jane. So I padded her ankles and secured the rope to them good and firmly and she set off head first down the shaft. I lowered her down quite slowly. When she called to me, I stopped her and let the other end of the rope down to her. She took an age to fasten the rope to him, working upside down in that confined space, and I only realized later that she'd had a nosebleed and been sick but she stuck at it, which many people wouldn't. At long last she called out to say that it was done and I could pull her up. It took all my strength but I managed it, and an awful sight she was, all bloodied. And, of course, being upside down her nosebleed had run up her forehead instead of down her face, which looked really weird. After that, at least there were two of us to pull him up, but we were both exhausted and he was inclined to jam in the narrow bits so that we had to let him down and pull him up again, so we had to do most of it more than once, and it seemed to take hours and hours but at least Jane's knots held. And when he was halfway up we got a call to say that help was on the way. The time the call took gained us a little bit of a rest. Then we made a real effort and brought him the rest of the way.

'He was an even worse sight than she was because, as I said, with hanging upside down she'd had a nosebleed to mix with his blood and she'd been sick on his head but, what was worst of all, he was hardly breathing. Somebody warned me once that one danger in giving the kiss of life is of damaging somebody's lungs by breathing too hard. I don't know if that's true or not but I was certainly puffing away as if I'd run a mile, so

Jane gave him the kiss of life for what seemed like ages.

'Mr Fellowes and Mr Grant had got the message I'd left with the police and they arrived at last, along with two ambulance men who brought a portable oxygen cylinder and a stretcher. That was more or less the end of my active role.'

Several of the journalists were trying to ask questions but Ian Fellowes retained control of the meeting. While Helena was speaking, one of the constables had come in and whispered to Luke. 'I have just received a message from the "New Royal",' Luke told the meeting. 'Roddy is intermittently recovering consciousness but so far he has shown no sign of recollecting anything later than when he left home to meet my great-granddaughter. My *other* great-granddaughter.'

There was a silence charged with puzzlement. 'That,' said Ian Fellowes, 'brings us to the other half of the story, the largely unknown half. The combination of a girl and a dog saving a boy in a rather spectacular fashion has overshadowed the fact that we don't know how he came to be down the well.' There was a fresh buzz of interest.

'He had no cause to be at Glenshuan that

we know of. He had a firm date with the older sister of Jane here and they had a plan for the evening and a table booked for dinner. What caused the change of plan?

'We know that he went to Kempfield. The manager of Kempfield, Mr Buckley, and the financial director, Mr Hopgood, were both present at Kempfield at the same time as the boy, according to the register; and Mrs Hopgood was seen to be waiting in Mr Hopgood's car outside the main door. Not one of the three has been seen since early the day before yesterday, the morning after the boy Roddy McWilliam failed to show up for his date, although we have been making every effort to contact them.

'I'm hoping that you or your viewers, readers or listeners will be able to help. Coincidence may be at work, or there may be banal explanations for both puzzles, but at first glance the happening of each makes the other seem more strange. I am not prepared to hypothesize at this stage. There are hundreds of possible explanations. I just want to know which one is true.'

Several hands were now waving frantically but Ian Fellowes soldiered on. 'Before we open the floor to discussion and questions, you had better know this. A major difficulty is that the CVs of Mr Buckley and Mr Hopgood seem to have been removed from the Kempfield files. Moreover, we do not have a single good photograph of any of the three absentees. Mr Grant has been a photographer working in this area for many years and concerned with Kempfield since its foundation. He has been through his digital records without success. In particular, he has studied crowd shots taken at events such as the opening of the new wing at Kempfield, events that the two senior members of the team could hardly avoid, but on any occasions when either of them was caught in shot the face is turned away or partly hidden by somebody or something else. That occurs too often to be coincidence. Accordingly a local artist, Miss Kemp, has been asked to piece together the portions of faces that we do have and to sketch in any missing pieces, aided by Mr Grant. He at least was acquainted with the two men and had glimpsed the lady. Photocopies of Mary Kemp's work will be available, but if anybody has photographs of the individuals we would be grateful for the use of them.' He nodded to Luke who turned to a video recorder and a large TV screen behind the speakers. Lifelike artwork of three faces appeared in turn, exchanging about every ten seconds.

'And now,' Ian said, 'I must thank you for your patience. We will now take questions or discussion.'

A reporter from the *Scotsman* managed to grab the first question, simply by being a very large man with a voice like a trumpeting elephant. 'Is it your theory that one or more of these people pushed the laddie down the well?'

Ian Fellowes had come across this particular man before and he could see a dozen dangers. He said, 'I am certainly not going to voice any such slander. Mr Kincaid knows very well that it is much too early for discussion of theories. It is equally possible that these three individuals happened on the same information or valuables as did the young man and therefore met with violence or intimidation. Or, as I said, maddening coincidence may be at work and the three may be perfectly innocent but not yet have returned from a long golfing break. If you or your public can shine any light we will be grateful.'

Discussion continued, seeming endless, but little emerged about the absent trio. The reporters turned their attention back to

Jane. A woman reporter from the *Scottish Sun* asked her whether there was any romance between her and Roddy.

Jane had been told to deny flatly any suggestion of anything amorous, but instead she said 'No comment.' She was in mischievous mood and well aware that this would provoke more interest.

'Is he in love with you?' the reporter persisted.

Luke opened his mouth to refer to Jane's youth – a factor that tended to be overlooked in the face of the maturity of her manner. Jane spoke first. 'You would have to ask him that,' she said, and on impulse she added, 'And then you could tell me what he says.'

When the friendly laughs had died away the reporter asked, 'Do you love him?'

Jane smiled complacently. 'No comment,' she said again.

'Why is the elder sister – Violet, is it? – why is she not present?' another woman reporter asked.

'Violet was very much upset, as I'm sure you can understand,' said Ian, 'and she didn't know more than the bare facts that you've been given. In fact, you have been given what in a court of law would be called

126

"best evidence". It was decided that she would be better off waiting for news at home along with the health visitor who is an old family friend. I understand that they have now gone into Edinburgh together to visit the patient. The doctors felt that such visits might perhaps aid the return of his memory and reassure them both that he was on the road to recovery.'

The discussion continued for nearly another hour. Questions flew, but Ian Fellowes had been unusually frank about what was known to the police and the others had said as much as they were prepared to divulge. The locals who had come, mostly out of nothing more than nosiness, recognized or thought that they recognized the subjects of Mary Kemp's drawings but only as faces passed in the street. Nobody had any hard facts to contribute except that the neighbours of the Hopgoods spoke of a regular traffic of visitors' cars and one lady mentioned being asked by a visiting driver for the way to Doctor Hopgood's house.

Ian Fellows drew the meeting firmly to a close. Jane had been becoming overexcited and Luke was anxious to get her home before she stepped further over the line and hinted at a passionate affair with Roddy

127

McWilliam. First it was necessary to recover Helena, who was so relieved to have got her public appearance behind her that she was easy meat for a trio of reporters who had carried her off to the small cocktail bar and plied her with brandy and lemonade.

They got to Luke's car by the expedient of ignoring the pestering reporters and walking through the middle of the throng as though deaf and blind, treading hard on any feet that were not withdrawn in time. They were halfway up the hill before the second round of drinks hit home and Helena began to sing. Unfortunately what she was singing was a version of an old song that had metamorphosed into *'Just a bonk at twilight'*. To Luke's relief Jane failed to hear precisely what it was that *'softly came and went'*.

Luke was slightly gruff as he helped Helena to bed. He was tired, but also the song, which had been a favourite of his late wife, reminded him of the passage of the years. And Helena had been evasive on the subject of just who had taught her the less polite version of the old song.

EIGHT

The pace of life, usually resembling a gentle trot, had become a mad gallop. At first it was the media. No rival stories had occurred to overshadow the role reversal of the girl going down the well to rescue the boy. (One politician had made an indecent proposal to his researcher, but because he had not lied about it there was little interest. A fire demolished an Elizabethan mansion, but nobody died and there was no suspicion of arson. A tiger attacked a zookeeper. It failed in its attempt to kill him but, as nothing much else seemed to be happening and there seemed to be some nebulous association between a rather large pussy and a story involving a journey down a well, some of them decided to run with it.) To fill their pages and screens there was an increasing preoccupation with the one story that combined courage, romance and a continuing mystery, and whatever was lacking they invented. Jane and, less intensely, Helena were pestered. Jane thought that it was all rather fun and was flattered and pleased to have her name coupled romantically with Roddy's. Luke had no very rooted objection as long as the interest resulted in repeat fees for his photographs of the activity around the wellhead. Violet was infuriated that it was her sister's name and not her own that was being bandied about in connection with Roddy's but she had to hide her feelings or be seen as a loser and a bad one.

Roddy was making a slow recovery. His memory remained incomplete. Violet was given leave of absence to visit him every day. Jane argued that, as his rescuer, she should be allowed off school and taken on visits, but she was overruled. At school she was an object of interest, sometimes referred to or even addressed as Pussy or Ding Dong. She blossomed in the extra attention.

Media interest in the rescue was kept simmering by the mystery of the absentees and their probable connection with the other mystery of how Roddy came to be in the well. Helena was left to field most of the questions, unanswerable though they were. She developed her own technique, already beloved by journalists, of uttering many words without quite saying anything. This left her free to deny any of the more positive statements attributed to her.

Detective Inspector Ian Fellowes, in addition to being plagued by similar enquiries, had the task of trying to produce explanations for both mysteries. After a week of frustration he sought Luke out at home. Luke was struggling to unscramble a tangle that Violet, in her state of distraction, had made of the computer index of his digital photographs and was grateful for the interruption. After a typical break in the weather, warmth and sunshine had returned and were behaving as though they had never been away, so Luke set two garden chairs on the terrace behind the house. Ian, being on duty, regretfully refused beer so the promise of a tray of coffee was obtained from Helena.

Ian looked around. The house was backed by grass and woodland. Luke had stubbornly refused to be a slave to his own garden, but some of the big trees that had dominated the house from the south had been replaced over the years with smaller, specimen trees, admitting both sunshine and colour. Some of those had been chosen for their flowers or foliage; others now supported climbing plants. Ian looked around and sighed. 'You have a lovely place here,' he said. 'This is almost my first chance for a week to sit and relax. It seems a shame but I'm going to have to stir things up.'

'How so?'

'My little team had been picking away at the mysteries without making any progress. There's no starting point, and it's not easy to find the way when you don't know where you're starting from. They're sending through a chief inspector to kick things along.'

'And your nose is out of joint?' Luke asked.

Ian stretched and put his feet up on the low wall that surrounded the terrace. 'Not very much. In fact, very little. They're sending Chief Inspector Laird. Honoria Laird.'

'Are they indeed?' Luke sat up straighter. He might be in his eighties and suffering from erectile dysfunction, but he could still appreciate a beautiful woman. 'She's been bumped up from inspector, then?'

'Yes. She's had several major successes. But I don't grudge it to her. I knew her when she was a sergeant locally – in fact, I poached her off the Met.'

'They call her Honeypot, don't they?'

'Some do, but she hates it. She was Honoria Potterton-Phipps before she married so the nickname was almost inevitable. Promotion may make life awkward for her. She ranks equal with her husband now and there's word that when Superintendent Blackhouse retires she'll be favourite to take over his job. She'd be bloody good at it, too. Trouble is, not many men can stand being bossed by their wives. That's if they recognize that it's happening. Luckily most of them don't.' Inspector Fellowes, who was quite unaware of the light touch on his reins, smiled complacently. 'Oh well! I came to ask you what feedback you've had on our three missing persons?'

'I was going to ask you the same question,' Luke said. 'Of course there's general gossip doing the rounds, but nobody seems to know more than that the three kept themselves to themselves. The men went off to business during the weekdays, nobody knows where so it was probably disreputable. They lived separately but not far apart, so the lady managed to keep house for both of them. She hardly seems to have done any shopping in Newton Lauder. Nobody's spoken to me except for one man who thinks he saw her in Peebles, but he rather thinks that the date was before the three of them went missing, so he isn't much help. I didn't even bother referring him to you.'

'He came to see me anyway,' Ian said disgustedly. 'Along with a thousand others. And the trouble is that you have to be polite and seem interested or the public stops bringing you their goodies. Every possible sighting has to be checked out. But ever since John Stonehouse did his disappearing act with all the publicity, the public has known how to obtain a false passport. Also there seems to have been a boom in the stolen passport business recently. So they could have dropped out of sight one at a time and hopped straight on a plane.'

Luke was struggling to envisage the problems that would have confronted three such fugitives. 'That presupposes that they knew that they might have to make a run for it. The Stonehouse method of getting a false passport entailed getting a copy of the birth certificate of a child who had died at about the right time. Died, because you had to be sure that the individual had never had a passport; the right time, because the apparent age had to correspond. That all takes time. So would waiting for a crooked dealer to come up with passports at least of the right gender and approximate age.'

'True. But we don't know what they've been up to, so we can only assume that they thought it urgent enough to warrant making preparations.' The detective inspector scratched his short, sandy hair, producing a sound rather like somebody walking through a stubble-field. 'The lady's small car is still in their garage but her husband's Volvo turned up in a multi-storey car park in Edinburgh. It had run out of time so I'm not even bothering to send someone to wait for them coming back.'

'It could be that they're still here, lying low,' Luke said.

'I'd like to think so. The one really helpful pointer is that the reports from the public of sightings of one or more of the trio come from all over Scotland, but I had pins stuck in a map in the hope that a distinct trail might show up. No such luck, but there was a small but definite cluster at Turnhouse Airport and one taxi driver who took three people out to the airport from that end of Princes Street thinks that he recognizes his fares in our composite pictures. The trouble is that he isn't quite sure whether they were coming or going.'

Luke's eyebrows went up but before he

could comment Helena came out through the French windows. The next few minutes were taken up with fetching another chair and another cup for her, pouring coffee for three and bringing her up to date. When she had caught up, she said, 'If coincidence isn't at work again, it sounds as though they're guilty of something serious. Did their house and his flat not give you any clues?'

Luke sighed. That was exactly what he had been about to say. He reminded himself to remain placid. In his old age he had developed a tendency to irritability. Usually he kept it firmly repressed but occasionally it surfaced. Helena often brought it out in him despite, or perhaps because of, having the best intentions. Their mutual awareness was such that she would sense what he needed next and produce it for him. All too often she would be handing him something that he would need but not yet, or while his hands were occupied; or, as now, anticipating what he had been about to say. He knew that he needed mothering and would need it more and more as time passed; and yet he resented the implication that he already needed a substitute mother to keep his thoughts in order as well as his cupboards and appearance.

Looking at her in a moment of revelation, he knew that he was being unfair. She was not so very much younger than he was but in a kind light she could have passed for his granddaughter. Age sat very lightly on her. She had retained both prettiness and femininity along with most of her figure only slightly blunted by time. And for some obscure, female reason she adored him. They had met when he dragged her out of her flooded car in a swollen burn, but to him that hardly seemed to be enough reason for blind adoration. He knew that he should be totally happy with their relationship. He was experiencing teenage rebellion seventy years late.

'This early in a case,' Ian Fellowes said, 'one mustn't forget any possibility, but at the moment I can't think of any way that they could all three be innocent. One of them, perhaps, being blackmailed or threatened by the others, but not all three. The assumption has to be that they've fled. But *why* remains a pivotal mystery. It took us until yesterday morning to persuade the sheriff that they really had fled the ... Excuse me.'

His mobile phone had sounded its peremptory summons. He keyed to receive the call and listened for some seconds before saying, 'Ask her if she'd mind coming here.' He listened to a small voice quacking in the police building at the bottom of the hill, then grunted and switched off. 'There's a lady at the nick, wants to speak to me personally. You don't mind if I see her here?

'To resume, yesterday my little team, with occasional interference from me, spent the day searching the two homes. Any signs of panic departure were uncertain, to say the least. By that I mean that there were examples of untidiness but little more than in an average dwelling. Most of the usual possessions were still there but it did seem that toiletries were in short supply and there were gaps among the clothes. No passports, travel documents or bankbooks were to be seen. We've uplifted such files as we came across but at first glance they seem to contain nothing but the most mundane and uninformative material. I conclude that they have known for a long time that they might have to do a disappearing act, but that is only a guess mixed with intuition and a touch of second sight aided by a crystal ball and tea leaves. If we only had one firm fact to use as a springboard...'

'If you want to talk it over again,' Helena

138

said, 'perhaps I can help.'

Luke ran all the known facts and the suppositions through his mental computer and isolated the one that seemed to be making faces at him. He caught Ian's eye and raised his eyebrows while indicating Helena by a tilt of his head. 'We were talking about the little room behind the office at Kempfield,' he said.

'No problem,' Ian said. 'You can tell Helena about it if you like.'

Luke was surprised but glad of the opportunity to let Helena struggle. 'There is one find that seems inexplicable,' he said. 'And when you get that, the inexplicable has an explanation that usually sits solidly in the middle of everything and furnishes a key to at least part of the mystery.' He saw that Ian was looking amused. 'You said that yourself,' he reminded the DI. 'Behind the office at Kempfield there's a small room that was intended to be used for filing. In this day and age, information is kept on computer or on computer-fed disks and tapes so that storage space becomes superfluous. The space had been used for some other purpose. It had been cleared out and furnished with a commonplace plastic-topped table. It seems to have been treated to another, 'hastier clearance.'

'There were some empty medicine bottles,' Ian said, 'blank labels, a saucer and sponge tainted with what the laboratory insists was once the kind of glue used for labels. And there were traces of white powder.'

'Make what you can of that,' Ian told Helena. He paused as the sound of a car reached them from the far side of the house. 'This will be the visitor. I hope that she may provide just what we need but I'm not holding my breath. May I bring her out here?'

Luke gave a small snort of amusement. 'You surely don't think that we're going to say no while we're seething with curiosity.'

Ian smiled. 'I didn't think any such thing. But I came here because you're the civilians most closely involved and because you've tapped into the local gossip for me in the past. People speak less freely when there's only a policeman present.'

While they were speaking, Helena had slipped away through the French windows. She knew too well that Luke was becoming too stiff to treat getting to his feet as a matter of only casual endeavour and Ian was too used to having juniors to wait on him to think, while mulling over his other preoccupations, of doing his own errands. She returned in less than a minute carrying, in one hand, another of the folding garden chairs, in the other a fourth coffee cup. She was followed by a lady who she introduced simply as Miss Flaxton. Helena seated herself firmly in one of the chairs and waited to be sent to sit out of earshot.

'I wished to see Detective Inspector Fellowes,' Miss Flaxton said firmly. The word *alone* was unspoken but definitely present. She was an upright lady of perhaps fifty years, in a smart and expensive business suit. She had not bothered with make-up and her skin was good enough not to show any lack of it; nevertheless, there could be no doubt that she was taking care of her appearance. Any grey had been coloured out of her dark hair. Her figure had definitely remained *de luxe*, with the aid of some modern corsetry, though Luke judged that it would not photograph well. (This remained his criterion for judging feminine looks.) She still presented an attractive picture except for a very firm jaw, which detracted slightly from her femininity and placed her firmly on the handsome rather than the pretty side of beauty.

'I am Inspector Fellowes,' Ian said. 'You

may see me alone if you wish. But I understand that you have something to say on the
matters raised at the press conference last
weekend. Mr and Mrs Grant are very much
involved and it seems very likely that I shall
wish to consult them.' Luke and Helena had
never married but, in deference to their
years, the fiction was preserved locally.

Miss Flaxton's glance passed over Helena
with only the recognizable flicker of hostility
of one still attractive woman for another.
But when she looked at Luke her gaze
steadied. Luke's memory had already been
stirred by a timbre in her voice. Now, in an
instant, he was transported back twenty
years or more.

Luke had always banked with the Scottish &
Borders Bank in Newton Lauder. Many
years earlier he had been in the habit of
visiting it, on average, once a week to draw
cash because the local hole-in-the-wall was
so badly situated as to be almost illegible
except at night or on totally overcast days.
For a month or two he had become aware of
a jolt whenever he made eye contact with a
dark-haired young teller. At such moments,
his eyes were inclined to linger and she
might pass a pink tongue over her lips. They

had never exchanged more than the most banal of banking words but her voice held promise and the sexual tension between them was beginning to vibrate.

At that time, Luke was not in any relationship; but nor was he looking to enter one. He loved women. He was delighted by all things feminine. He was relieved that he had not been born one, because he rather thought that women had had slightly the worse of the bargain, but he was enchanted by legs in nylon; soft, round buttocks and full, red lips; even the female way of thinking that, to a man, could seem so upside-down, pleased him. (To a man, the idea of making it a principle that your very prettiest clothing should never be seen, lacked logic. He had once, when the French were at the height of one of their demonstrations against British produce and in a moment when he had not been noticeably sober, shocked a crowded room into silence by remarking loudly that he could forgive the French for inventing myxomatosis in return for their greatest invention – the suspender belt.) Women usually responded to his looks, which had matured with age, to his reputation for sustained virility and to his evident admiration. However, not even a pair of full and jaunty breasts or the whisper of silk beneath the severe suit would have him paying court to a young woman with a forceful jaw, a proud nose and freckles.

Early one summer's evening he was returning from the shops, heading for home through a street of mixed houses and flats. A furniture van was blocking half the road. He pulled across to his right to let an oncoming car go by. Very few human figures were to be seen but beyond the furniture van he glimpsed somebody who looked very like the sexy teller from the bank. She was looking in his direction. When he was able to pull out and pass the furniture van, he saw the girl sprawled on the pavement beside what he took to be her car. As he approached she sat up and waved to him.

He drew up, of course. He could hardly do less. The fact that a great deal of exquisite leg was on display and not a little pale pink knicker had nothing to do with it. He dismounted and asked whether he could help.

'So silly of me,' she said. 'I seem to have sprained my ankle. Can you help me into my house, please. That one.' She pointed.

He pulled her to her feet and she leaned on him. Synchronizing a walk and a hop proved extremely difficult. He looked around but there was nobody to help or even to care. Stooping, he picked her up. She was lighter than he had expected. He had intended to take her under the knees but she moved as he lifted her and he caught her under the thighs, bypassing her thin summer skirt. She did not seem to mind very much. She contrived to unlock the front door while still in his clasp. 'Upstairs, if you can manage it,' she said. 'I'd be better lying flat and my mother won't be back for hours yet.'

Luke was not ready to admit that he could not manage to carry a lightweight girl up a flight of stairs. He had performed the feat often in the past, for social rather than humanitarian reasons. He had to turn and climb sideways to avoid hitting her head on the banisters, but as he began the climb she turned and gave a small wriggle while straightening slightly. She slipped again and her silken bottom was in his hand. Her perfumed breath was in his ear. He entered by the door she indicated and lowered her gently on to the bed. He then found that his hand was gripped between her thighs.

There was no doubt now what she had in mind and Luke was too much of a gentleman to thwart a lady. The occasion might have been very special if her mother had not made an unexpectedly early return and walked in on them.

Very shortly thereafter, when he came to take his leave, she no longer showed any trace of a limp.

The books of etiquette have little to say about how two people should comport themselves when meeting again some years after sharing or almost sharing the delights of the bedchamber. There are those who would make no sign of recognition, others who might greet with cries of joy and air kisses. Some might feel reproaches more suited to the occasion. Luke, after more than half a century of close encounters of the amorous kind, was not inexperienced in dealing with that contingency and he usually took his lead from the other person. If she wished to pretend that they had never met before, he would not feel insulted.

Miss Flaxton met his eye but gave no other sign of recognition. So be it.

Ian Fellowes said, 'The boy who fell or was pushed into the well was the boyfriend of Mr Grant's great-granddaughter. His other great-granddaughter was lowered head first down the well to rescue him.'

'And how is the boy?' Miss Flaxton enquired politely without showing any depth of interest.

'He is making progress but his memory is still affected,' said Ian.

'I see. So naturally you want to know all you can learn about the three missing people. I saw the broadcast but it was only when I saw the Identikits, or whatever they were, in my local paper that I realized that I had seen the older man before. Hopgood, I believe he's calling himself now, but I knew him as Craven. I used to work in the local bank,' she explained without giving the least hint that Luke would know that fact, though he was sure that she had recognized him. 'I was studying for my degree in accountancy in those days. I work for McInnes and Isaacson, the accountants in Dunbar, now. But while I was still with the bank here, Mr Craven asked for a confidential appointment with me. Why he picked on me I don't know, except perhaps because he had made some unimportant enquiry about the state of his wife's bank account and I had refused to let him have it without his wife's authorization. That may have satisfied him that I don't talk out of school.

'He wanted to know about foreign countries. In particular, he wanted to know what the position would be if he retired abroad and took his money with him. If he returned here or changed domicile again, would he be able to move his money?

'That's a question that arises quite often. Somebody retires abroad in search of sunshine, but eternal sunshine can be tiresome and they come to resent the difficulties of language and differences of culture. When they give up and want to come home, countries that once welcomed their money are less keen to see it exported again. I explained that, while I could answer his questions as at that morning, in fluctuating economic circumstances countries are inclined to move the goalposts. His best bet would be to move his money and establish one or more accounts in some safe banking country – Liechtenstein and Holland came first to mind but there are others. He could then move lesser sums to wherever he was living at the time. I told him how to do it and how to start. He seemed grateful. In fact he wanted to pay me a fee, but that would have been against the bank's rules.'

'Did he take your advice?'

'I believe so. I certainly noticed that his bank accounts, which had held substantial sums, were suddenly emptier than ever before.'

'Which country did he choose?' Ian's voice had become husky.

'I haven't the faintest idea. I believe that I also mentioned Switzerland and one or two others. The bank might still be able to trace a record, but if he took my advice there might not be a trail to follow. In these days of identity theft, people often prefer not to leave a trail, paper or electronic, behind their money.'

Ian's expression would have been suited to someone who suspected that his latest *escargot* was in fact a slug. 'He didn't give any indication as to which country he had in mind?'

'I'm afraid not. I changed jobs not long after that.'

Ian spoke slowly. It was evident that he was thinking hard. 'Before that ... Do you recollect anything ... any transaction that might suggest ... what he was doing for a living and where he was doing it?'

Miss Flaxton looked at him as though he had lost his mind. 'Good Lord, no! Banking nowadays is highly mechanized. A client presents a cheque for paying in and the machine reads the magnetic number and identifies the account of the payer. The only manual efforts are keying in the amount and identifying the account of the payee. It would be unusual for any bank staff to notice the source of the payment unless it happened to be conspicuous for some reason. If it's any help, I have a faint impression that most of the payments into his account, at least the ones that I handled, came from a single source, possibly a solicitor or some agency.'

'Were they large sums?' Ian asked.

'I don't remember any details but my general recollection is of very substantial sums on deposit. The payments in were regular, not earth-shaking but definitely not to be sneezed at.'

Ian Fellowes blew out a breath and glanced round the others for help.

Helena rose to the challenge. 'When he started to ask questions about which countries he might be able to get his money out of, it would be logical to start by asking about a particular place. I mean, I can't visualize him asking vaguely, "Which countries could I get my savings back from?" but I can easily imagine him saying "Would it be easy to bring my money back from Momboland?" You follow me?'

'Oh yes. I follow you,' said Miss Flaxton. She frowned but not enough to crease her forehead. 'I have a vague idea that Portugal was mentioned. When I think about that discussion, I don't hear any words but I think Portugal and see a map of the Iberian Peninsula. It's very vague and I wouldn't swear to it in court.'

'I don't suppose you'll ever have to,' Ian Fellowes said gloomily.

'If that's all,' Miss Flaxton said, 'I'll get back to earning a living. But I'll leave you my card. It has my home and office phone numbers on it, my Fax number and my email address, so if you think of any more questions you should be able to get hold of me.' When she used the words 'get hold' her eyes were locked with Luke's.

'I think we could manage that,' Ian said.

NINE

Luke saw Miss Flaxton to her car. Her only acknowledgement of their earlier near-relationship was to allow him a more than passing glimpse of her legs as she settled into the driver's seat. It did very little for him but he accorded her a grateful smile. Women, he had found, appreciate these little acknowledgements. On the terrace, he found Helena and Ian picking over the latest scraps of information. 'At least we know that they're almost certainly abroad,' Ian said. 'Probably Spain or Portugal. Not that it helps very much. We'll still have to circulate all forces and the national computer (commonly known as God) with an enquiry and we still don't even know what they've done. Another whadiddydo, in fact. They're the worst. If you're investigating an incident you have a starting point. The facts are there to be found. But if you don't know what you're looking for your chances of finding it are greatly reduced.'

Luke settled himself comfortably into his chair. 'You should know a little more when you've taken the next step,' he said. 'If they were making preparation to escape abroad, they must have known that they were going to step outside the law.'

Ian was relaxing, slumped in the garden chair with his feet up on the low wall that bordered the terrace. 'That's true,' he said. 'But if they gained client status the lawyer won't talk.'

Helena was looking lost. 'The next step? What's the next step? I mean, they'd already stepped outside the law, dealing in drugs.'

Luke gave a small snort of laughter. 'Ian's been playing games with us. He was looking amused when we discussed the white power. I think he was watching us go wandering up a blind alley.'

Helena turned the eyes of a hurt spaniel on Ian. 'Is that right?'

Ian let his laughter show. 'On analysis, the white powder turned out to be a mixture of icing sugar and fine flour. And you may be comforted to know that we were fooled just as much as you were. We spent a day chasing up drug suppliers and possible dealers without getting a sniff – there's an appropriate metaphor for you!'

'But why would they be doing – what? – mixing those white powders together and filling small medicine bottles?'

'Is it just possible,' Luke said slowly, 'that they were pulling off a scam prior to buzzing off abroad? They could have been telling customers that it was heroin or cocaine, or even some new drug that has a quite different appearance.'

'We didn't get a hint of anything like that,' said Ian. 'What's more, if somebody was selling or pretending to sell hard drugs, the very last thing he'd do would be to label them. No, I think that's just what you called it, a dead end. We'll come back to it whenever we get a lead but for the moment it goes on the back burner, to change metaphors again. So what else were they doing?'

'Think about it,' said Luke. 'They're making contingency plans to get their money abroad. They were asking about moving it back again – in case their crimes did not come out after all, I'd suppose. If they didn't already have several passports each in different names they'd need to get them. They wouldn't have time to do it like John Stonehouse, requesting copies of the birth certificates of babies who'd died in infancy about the right number of years ago. They'd need to contact a dealer in stolen and forged passports. There can't be so many specialists in that field.'

Although slumped in his chair, Ian managed a shrug. 'But almost any dealer in stolen goods would buy and resell a passport if it came his way. What else would they want to know?'

Helena shrugged.

Ian snapped his fingers. 'Extradition,' he said. 'They'd want to be sure which countries do or don't have extradition treaties with Britain or the EU or whatever.'

'Extradition law's very complex and hedged about with exceptions,' Luke said. 'Cases are going through courts all the time. In their shoes, I think I'd make my choice on other grounds but be ready to move again quickly at any sign of trouble. I'll tell you something else. I wouldn't want to leave a back trail by consulting a lawyer. I think he could get what he needs to know off the Internet. Did either of them leave a computer behind?'

'You're absolutely right. He did indeed.' Ian's face brightened and then dulled again. 'Buckley did. A big, old-fashioned sit-up-and-beg desktop. But he probably had a laptop and took it with him.' He sighed and got to his feet. 'I was getting to enjoy being able to sit still for a change. I'd better go and get an expert to look at the one he left behind and the Kempfield office one as well. It takes a lot more to eradicate material completely from a computer than most people think. Most of the time the thing you thought you'd deleted is still there, waiting until it's superseded by later material. I'll pay you another call tomorrow if I may.'

'Any time,' Luke said. 'Within reason,' he added quickly.

Helena saw Ian to his car and came back but she did not sit down. 'You had an affair with her, didn't you?' she said.

Luke's mind darted around. Laugh it off? Flat denial? Deny it unconvincingly to let a little jealousy spice their life together? But no. Helena might take to that game with a little too much enthusiasm. 'It was a long, long time ago,' he said, 'and it was unconsummated. Her mother came home unexpectedly. It was one of the most embarrassing events in my life. I never met her again except across the counter in the bank.'

'And you're not still hankering to make up the deficiency?'

'Frankly, I hadn't thought about her for years. I don't even know how many.'

'Good answer,' said Helena. 'I'll see if I can't make it up for you tonight.'

Roddy McWilliam had been making progress towards recovery but this suddenly ceased or even slightly reversed. The doctors made soothing noises and spoke mostly in Latin, which are two of the signs of breakers ahead. Roddy was scheduled for further though less major surgery designed, insofar as they could penetrate the medical jargon and obfuscation, to remove a remaining blood clot that had refused to be dispersed by medication. Violet would not be able to see him for at least a day.

This came as a relief to Helena. The helpful health visitor could not continue indefinitely transporting Violet to and fro. The bus service, such as it was, ran at all the wrong times and there were no longer any trains. Helena was reluctant to undertake the duties of the chauffeur but Violet was determined to visit every day. It was certain that sulks or tantrums, or possibly both, would follow if Helena reneged on the insincere offer that she had made in a moment when Violet was at her most apprehensive. For the moment, life could return almost to its usual, ordered rhythm.

157

Luke was equally relieved. He could have managed without his car for a few days, by hiring from Ledbetter's Garage if anything urgent turned up. In the absence of its manager and financial director, the Kempfield Centre was almost running itself but when policy decisions were required Luke, as the nearest member of the committee, was increasingly being called on. At home, he could usually agree to act if the papers were brought to him or, if his presence was unavoidable, insist on being fetched. Against this, he had converted satisfactorily, some said brilliantly, to digital photography and could manage all the editing entailed, but he had never been really comfortable with the cyberworld. He had, after all, been in the army when the computer was in its infancy and well into middle age before it came into general use. The indexing and cross-indexing of his photographs had become marvellously efficient by computer but a real pain for one to operate who was almost computer-illiterate as well as fumble-fingered with a keyboard. His one hope was that Jane would come to match Violet's computer skills before Violet left the family home – if he should live so long.

When Inspector Ian Fellowes made his

return visit, Violet, still burying her resentment, had gone out with Jane and Circe, intending to visit the place of Roddy's descent into the well. Jane was not averse to the chance to strut a little. Helena was making a rush at the housekeeping because, unless Roddy suddenly turned the corner or Violet's employer lost patience with the absence of his apprentice, her days for the foreseeable future were likely to be spent in the driving seat of Luke's car. She could only hope that Luke and Jane between them would try very hard to cope. Luke was printing a series of *risqué* glamour shots commissioned for a calendar by a tyre manufacturer, using images that he had taken for an earlier series and never used. Fashions might change but the client's taste in models and their adornment remained constant. At the same time, he was waiting with limited patience for Violet to return and finish updating the index of his huge library of shots, half of which was still in manuscript and half on computer. They had finished Section Three (Glamour) and were due to start Section Four (Wildlife). Jane insisted that there was only the haziest of boundaries between the two.

Years earlier, Luke could have pored

indefinitely over carefully lit and posed shots of nubile young ladies in or near the altogether, but he was an old man now. Sexual arousal did not occur at the drop of a silken garment. On the other hand, as he grew older he found himself less intrigued by stories of crime. He had sometimes been called out to take photographs of crime scenes for the police, who found it cheaper on occasions to employ a local photographer than to keep a full complement of staff and pay for their travelling and idle time. The sight of injuries and death and the tears of those affected soon lost their interest and their appeal and became no more than reminders of his own mortality. But at the sound of Ian's car the computer was shut down and he coaxed himself to his feet. They seated themselves once again on the terrace.

The day was cooler, the sunlight softer, the birdsong sweeter. The forecast was not good, but Luke said that that was almost a guarantee of sunshine. Weather forecasts, he said, were about as reliable as a politician's promise. 'It seems a pity to talk about murder on a day like this,' he said, 'but I suppose that that's the reason for your call?' He was tempted to give the inspector an exploration of his morning's work, but he had used that trick once before to distract the other from the grimmer face of policework and it could not be counted on to work again.

'I'm afraid so,' Ian said. 'I want to bring you up to date and find out if you can help me forward again.'

'All right,' Luke said resignedly. 'Tell me all about it.'

'There's not a great deal to tell. You already know most of it. Sometimes I feel as if I'm trying to run through syrup. Every likely looking opening slams shut in my face. We know about the local bank accounts, but they're remarkably uninformative. Clearly there were other accounts elsewhere, or even here but in different names. In these days of telephone and Internet banking, it's become quite easy to open and close accounts in fictitious names.

'Hopgood's computer had been used to access the Internet. He had, as we supposed, been looking up extradition, but all that shows up is a general summary of international law without a clue to individual countries.

'Phone-calls are still coming in from people who've seen our appeal in the media.' As if on cue, the mobile phone in his

161

pocket trilled a little tune. He listened, acknowledged a message and signed off. 'I'll have to go,' he said. 'A visitor who says that he has vital information, which probably only means that he saw somebody vaguely resembling one of the trio, he's not sure where or when. It's turning into that sort of case. And I was hoping that I could come up with some fresh ideas if we kicked it around for a while. I'll be back.'

Luke had recovered, for the moment, his curiosity about the missing trio. 'Ask your visitor to come here,' he suggested.

'But—'

'There weren't any buts the other day,' Luke pointed out.

'Miss Flaxton mentioned your name, I don't know why.'

Luke could have made a good guess but he decided not to open that particular can of worms. 'I may be able to help some more,' he said.

Ian Fellowes called his office back and after a short argument and a much longer explanation as to how the visitor should find Luke's house, agreement was reached. Ian put his phone away and resumed. 'There was one more thing we got out of the computer. One of hundreds but this one may or may not be significant. He had been calling up dictionaries, but most of those were some time ago. The most recent was a Portuguese dictionary. It didn't happen very often, so it may not mean much.'

'Or it may mean that he's familiar enough with the language not to have to look in the dictionary very often,' Luke pointed out.

Ian frowned in thought. 'You could be right,' he said. 'Not that it takes us much further. Portugal's a big country and their police have methods that are foreign to us. They're very secretive. I don't see my chiefs authorizing an approach when we don't even know what the trio have – or has – done.'

They were in danger of getting into an argument as to whether a trio was singular or plural. Luckily the route from the police building to Luke's house only entailed a drive up the hill and a turn into a side road for a quarter-mile. They very soon heard the sound of a car. Luke was embarking on the struggle to rise – he seemed to get stiffer every day – when he was saved the trouble. Helena appeared in the French windows. 'I was in the hall anyway,' she said. 'This is Mr Blantyre. He says that you're expecting him.' She disappeared again.

163

Ian Fellowes jumped to his feet with a nimbleness that Luke could only envy. He performed the necessary introduction. 'Mr Grant had an interest in this case and I am also picking his brains.'

'There's not much to pick at the moment,' Luke said. 'We seem to be rather at a loss. Perhaps you can give us a better starting point.'

'Well, I'll try,' Mr Blantyre said. His pinstripe suit was an unwise choice for one of his figure. He was a stout little man with a red face, silver hair and a jolly expression. He seemed rather inclined to sweat. He lowered himself carefully into the proffered chair. 'It's a wonder that I ever saw the pictures in the papers,' he said. 'I don't watch telly much. I live at Carnwath, over towards Lanark. I'm a physiotherapist. I take private patients at home and one of them left a copy of your local rag in the sitting room that I use for waiting. I picked it up to throw it away and there, staring me in the face – literally, because you know how eyes in a picture can follow you around – was the story of that brave little girl—'

'My great-granddaughter,' Luke said proudly.

'Really? – and how you wanted to know

more about those three people. I can't be absolutely sure, of course – they're not very good pictures – but I'm fairly sure.' (Ian looked as though for two pins he would clutch his brow. It seemed that the cup was to be dashed from his lips again.) 'The circumstances,' Mr Blantyre resumed, 'are so odd that it seemed worth bringing to your attention.

'Not far from Carnwath there's a big house, Yardstone House. It stands in open country and it had been empty for several years. It was taken over about three years ago as a nursing home. More of a hospice, really, because it specializes in care for wealthy cancer patients. It's all very confidential, but I'm called in sometimes to give treatments. Having cancer is no prophylactic against arthritis. The junior staff is all local and word goes around. It's run day-to-day by a doctor who was squeezed out of private practice because, frankly, he was never very clever at diagnosis, but he seems to be having some successes with treatment.' He paused.

'Go on,' Ian Fellowes said.

'I was wondering how to explain. Some of the patients saw your appearance on TV and there was some whispering. Those pictures

would not have been good enough to identify an individual, but three people together
is a bit too much of a coincidence. The
patients don't want to rock the boat, because sometimes they can get treatment that
isn't available to the NHS. But three people,
two men and a woman, appeared regularly
in the background until very recently. They
were generally believed to be the proprie-
tors. They weren't known by the names you
mentioned on the box. The younger man,
who you called Buckley, was called Burn-
side then and he was a surgeon – qualified
or not I wouldn't know, but he certainly
carried out surgical operations. The other
man, you called him Hopewell or Hopkins,
was sometimes addressed as Doctor.'

'It does sound as though these might be
the three characters who vanished suddenly
from here,' Ian Fellowes said uncertainly.
'I'd better pay this Yardstone House a visit.'

'I don't believe they've been seen around
Yardstone House for a week or two,' Mr
Blantyre said.

'That could fit. And you've no idea where
they've vamoosed to?'

Mr Blantyre produced the smirk of one
preparing to lay down a straight flush. 'I
didn't say that. I didn't say that at all. I can't

tell you the place or even the country but I may be able to help you to pin it down. It was general knowledge that they had links with another establishment somewhere abroad. It sometimes happened that a patient was known to be on his or her last legs and it would be suggested to that patient that it would be possible to give them better care and a happier end in warm sunshine and among flowers. I was kept waiting once while Hopewell—'

'Hopgood,' said Luke.

'– while Mr Hopgood was talking to a patient who was to receive physiotherapy. "I'm sure you'll be comfortable there," he was saying. "Flowers all round the year and the wine is very good." That patient disappeared from my patient list within a week.'

'But you can't say where?' Ian persisted.

'Now, I didn't say that,' Mr Blantyre said almost playfully. 'When I drove over here I expected to tell you that I hadn't the faintest idea. But things have changed.'

Luke had never seen Ian Fellowes blow his top, but he had a rich expectation that this was about to happen. Mr Blantyre, however, could see the same signs and a physiotherapist may develop a special talent for muscle-reading. 'I'll tell you how,' he said quickly.

'Coming through your hall, Mr Grant, I saw a large, framed, colour photograph of a place I didn't recognize but it looks rather like a Mediterranean harbour. When Mr Hopgood was coaxing Mr Menzies – that was the patient's name – Mr Hopgood had a brochure in his hand and that same photograph was on the back of it. There!'

Ian Fellowes had been disappointed before. He was not averse to looking gift horses in the mouth. 'How sure are you that it was the same photograph?' he asked.

'About as sure as one can be. I'm sure in my mind that it's the same place and the same picture and, to make sure, there's a young woman shown on the harbour wall. She's more or less wearing what almost qualifies as a scarlet bikini and her figure...' Mr Blantyre paused and looked sly. Evidently deciding that in all-male and non-medical company he could be frank he resumed, 'I would give her a massage any day and not charge her a penny. In fact, quite the reverse. She was in the photograph on that brochure and she's in the picture hanging on your wall.'

Some guarded questions revealed that Mr Blantyre, though prepared to talk endlessly, had nothing further of value to reveal.

TEN

Ian Fellowes was bursting to ask Luke the origin of that photograph and Luke was equally eager to tell him; but patience is the very hub of a detective's life and a valuable part of a photographer's. Any attempt at further discussion might have entailed triggering another outburst of circumlocution from Mr Blantyre, so they held their peace until that equally curious individual had given up lingering and, disdaining to ask the direct question, decided to take his leave. The other two hurried him through the hall and to his car and watched him drive away with a certain relief.

'Not even if I were in agony,' Ian Fellowes said as they re-entered the house, 'would I allow that man to lay a finger on me.'

Luke grunted agreement. 'He might set out to mend my leg and end up talking it off me.'

They stopped in the hall. The walls were adorned with a sprinkling of colour prints, mostly of scenery, but people and buildings and wildlife all had a share. Many of Luke's favourite shots found their place here and were regularly replaced as still more exciting, photogenic or fresher subjects came his way. The largest space was occupied by a print on the largest colour paper normally available. It showed a harbour where fishing boats jostled with pleasure craft. In the background tall, sunlit buildings climbed a steep hillside. Despite the size of the enlargement the detail was still razor sharp except for a slight smearing of people or vehicles that had been in motion.

'Madeira,' Luke said. 'Of course! That makes sense. It's a small island as islands go but there's remarkably little crime, so the Investigation Branch – I think they call it the P.J. for no reason that I can think of – isn't exactly overrepresented. I took this shot for inclusion in a hotel brochure, but it turned out so well that I sold it to the council for a poster.'

'I seem to remember that you have connections in Madeira.'

'I suppose you could call them connections. Let's go back and sit down – my knees begin to give me hell if I stand for too long.' When they were seated again on the terrace,

Luke resumed. 'It's only in the hotel and leisure complex business that I have any connections. Donkey's years ago, the original Senhor Bustini was buying the Waterside Hotel. He had started life as a fisherman but he had a talent for business. He gave up the fishing, borrowed some money and built a hotel. That was the start of a whole chain of hotels, mostly five-star, all over the world but principally Madeira.

'He was already well established when he bought the Waterside Hotel, not very far from here.'

'I know it quite well but I'd like to know it better,' Ian said. 'I take Deborah there to dinner whenever we're feeling rich. Go on.'

'The Senhor brought his daughter and his male secretary with him. I can guess what the attractions were. The daughter was intelligent and articulate and her English was good but she was certainly no oil painting, yet it turned out that she was pregnant by the secretary. If that fact had emerged while they were at home I rather think that a hit man might have been imported from Spain or Italy – the Portuguese are sticklers for family honour. It may just have been to relieve his feelings while they waited for the hit man that the old chap insisted that they went through an immediate marriage but perhaps I'm wronging him. I was photographing the hotel building so Senhor Bustini also engaged me to take wedding photographs but he made his attitude clear – it was that somebody had better take a few snaps so that he could show that a marriage had taken place. I was sorry for the pair. The bridegroom was terrified – he was certain to lose his job and he'd be lucky if that was all that he'd lose – and the girl was near hysteria; but I calmed them down, tidied them up, added a little make-up, took a lot of trouble with the lighting and background, chose the best angles and coaxed them into looking as though they loved each other dearly and it really was the happiest day of their lives. I even borrowed the bouquet from another wedding that I had covered the previous day, partly so that she could use it to hide the bump that was beginning to show.

'When I delivered the photographs to him, Senhor Bustini looked stunned. Though I say it myself, I'd got the pair of them looking very respectable and as though they were both looking forward to their bridal night, with no hint of having anticipated it. Months later, when the baby had made its appearance the old boy came to dote on his grandson and became quite happy to introduce the couple everywhere. He had been a one-man band but he began to trust more and more management in their hands and when he popped his clogs the bridegroom took the Bustini name and ended up as managing director with his wife as chair and major stockholder. The group of companies has gone on from strength to strength and the Bustinis are still convinced that I swung it for them. Well, maybe I did and maybe I didn't, it's what they believe that counts and I wouldn't do anything to change their minds.'

Ian Fellowes had been nodding slowly. The two had known each other and collaborated in the past and he knew that when Luke was well launched there was little point in trying to interrupt. But now he recognized what in TV circles is known as a 'natural break'. It was his chance and he seized it. 'I seem to remember you being flown out there on occasions to photograph hotels.'

Luke had been working towards certain favourite anecdotes and the old do not appreciate being interrupted. 'It has happened,' he said stiffly.

'There was also an occasion when you promoted an excuse to be flown out there so that you could make enquiries of a witness on my behalf.'

'That was rather different. We were looking into the death of my granddaughter-in-law, the mother of the two girls. I had to know what had happened.'

'True. And if you need motivation to look into how your future great-grandson-in-law came to be down a well—'

'Now, hold your horses. I don't need added motivation,' Luke said irritably. 'And you're making a giant leap to conclusions that even the two people most involved probably haven't got round to thinking about yet. Damn it, I've probably put more time in on this mystery than you have. But if you go there, the State pays your fare and subsistence.'

Ian sneered at him. 'Come on,' he said. 'Now who's living in a dream world? All that we have at the moment is a fragment of hearsay and some inspired guesswork. You know that there isn't a cat's chance in a boarding kennels of my fare being paid to Madeira on such shaky grounds. I don't believe for a moment that, on the basis of what we've got so far, they'd agree to

174

approach the Madeiran police and I'm damn sure that if they did so our targets would be up and gone within a day or two. And you've just finished telling me, not for the first time, how the Bustini family adores you for the brilliance of your wedding photographs.'

'In point of fact,' Luke, only a little molli-fied, said with dignity, 'I hadn't finished telling you, but you interrupted me before I could say that I'm sure that I've exhausted their goodwill by now.'

For a moment Ian Fellowes let a look of guile show through his habitual screen of ingenuousness. 'So sure that you'll promise me that the next time you go on a freebie to a Bustini luxury hotel in some subtropical paradise you'll take me along as your guest or valet or some such?'

That was pushing it too far. 'You should be so lucky,' Luke said.

Fellowes pointed a finger, pistol fashion, between Luke's eyes. 'I've got you there! Anyway, Honeypot will be here tomorrow and I'd like to be able to show her some progress. Would you at least email your friend Senhor Bustini and ask whether, if you were to email him photographs of the three pictures, he could have one of his dogsbodies ask around anyone who owes or is looking for favours from the hotel chain?'

'I could go that far,' Luke said. 'Not as far as Madeira, I don't mean that, but as far as sending that email.'

'Well, tell them to be discreet. The signs so far are that the fugitives think and plan ahead. If they were prepared enough to leave here at short notice they've almost certainly made much the same preparations again. We don't want them bolting by fishing boat. Madeira's within easy reach of too much of Africa and America, Canary Islands, the Caribbean—'

'All right,' Luke said. 'All right. Point taken.'

Chief Inspector Honeypot, Luke learned, was delayed for several days because she was called to give evidence in a case that had moved faster than expected (one of the participants had pled guilty, to the consternation of his accomplices). A weekend then intervened which she devoted to her own affairs except for taking the opportunity to visit Roddy in hospital and hear what little he remembered of the events. Monday then came and went while she was acquainted with the known facts, shown over the

Kempfield Creative Adventure Centre and was taken to see the well down which Roddy had so nearly vanished forever.

Luke was too busy to worry about her comings and goings at the time. Whoever had picked the main entrance door lock at Kempfield had repeated his unauthorized entry. This time, however, he had gone further and taken a chisel to the door of the little room behind the office. He had not made much impression on this because the door had been backed by another of solid oak. Luke was called on, not only as a member of the committee but as a photographer, using, in case he lost it, an old camera to which he attached little or no value. A camera trap was devised, hidden in a box file, and set.

Thus it was the Tuesday before DCI ('Honeypot') Laird and DI Fellowes came to visit. Luke was given to understand that this particular mountain was coming to the Prophet in deference to his age and frailty. He had just returned from walking Circe – a duty that had fallen back to him in the absence of anybody else to undertake it. In the past he had enjoyed his dog-walks but stiffening limbs had removed some of the joy. He disposed hastily of his boots. He could foresee certain advantages in being seen as a poor old cripple.

Luke rather suspected that the reason for having the interview on his home turf was not his age, which was not so very great in the changing demographics of the time, although he had found the arrival of his great-granddaughters to walk the Labrador that he had at the time a relief. (During his seventies he had considered himself no more than late middle-aged but as his eighties began to fall behind him he acknowledged, but strictly to his secret self, that he was getting on a bit.) The real reason was, he thought, rather that Ian Fellowes had begun to take an almost proprietorial interest in the beauty of the setting of Luke's house and wanted to show it off. He had begun to look at vacated farmhouses on his own behalf.

Luke had just got rid of his coat and boots when Ian's car approached.

Honeypot was impressed by the charming old house and garden and was generous enough to say so. They took seats out on the terrace. Luke was equally impressed. He had glimpsed her once in the distance without gaining more than an impression. Now, seen close up, he realized that the impression of beauty had not been an illusion but a reality deriving from perfect bone structure, meticulous attention to fitness and an impeccable sense of style. The effect would have been overpowering if she had shown any of the arrogant self-confidence that beautiful women commonly show. She was slim although she moved with a muscular grace. Luke, who knew his way around a beautiful woman, would have liked to put at least part of her beauty down to grooming. The availability of money had not been a hindrance. He had heard that her father was very wealthy and he could see that she was expensively dressed and made-up. Her hair had recently been through the salon of one of the top hairdressers – he could have made a reasoned guess as to which. But he was expert enough to see that these extravagancies counted for nothing. Dressed in sackcloth, pulled backwards through a hedge and with her hair full of twigs she would still have turned just as many heads. She could, he thought, have been a model; and he found out later that that had indeed been her first job after she left finishing school.

They exchanged the necessary civilities. Her manner could have been social rather than professional. Then she came down to the nitty-gritty. On the table – which was a single large round of elm, thickly varnished, supported by three roughly matching boulders – she placed a small tape recorder from her shoulder bag and switched it on. She recorded the date, time, place and those present and then led Luke through his personal knowledge of the events.

Luke finished by asking whether it was an appropriate moment to mention that an email had reached him from Madeira that morning.

'You've mentioned it and we'll see it later. The boy seems to be recovering well,' she said.

Luke began to revise his opinion as to Honeypot's lack of arrogance but he replied without heat. 'He is but his memory is not. I'm told that this sometimes happens in the case of a head injury and that it is the events immediately before the damage occurred that are likely to be recovered last, if at all. So we may never know how he came to be down the well.'

Honeypot's sensuous jaw and – he had to admit it to himself – kissable lips took on a firmer line. 'We'll know,' she said. 'Sooner or later, we'll know. We'll just have to get there by a less direct route. I think I've got the full picture now, such as it is, except that your pictures of the missing trio aren't very good.'

'They were composites from several different photographs and the light was different each time,' said Luke.

Honeypot nodded. 'Your artist did his best – her, was it? – but I'd like to see the originals that she was working from. I have a suspicion that I might know who they are if I wasn't being distracted by the bits that your artist put in by guesswork.'

Ian began to rise. 'I can fetch them.'

'I doubt if you could find them,' said Luke. 'In the absence of Violet, who does most of my filing for me, I'm not sure that I can find them either, but I'll try.' He pulled himself to his feet.

'Take your time,' Honeypot said. 'I've had rather a hard few days and I could sit here for hours, just letting the peace of it sink in.'

'Shall I bring tea? Or coffee?'

'Tea for me, please,' Honeypot said, with a smile so angelic that Luke felt the old hormones stir. While the kettle boiled he searched for the envelope in which the original photographs had been returned to him. The kettle clicked off just as he found it under a clutter of other prints. He carried the tray out through the French windows with the envelope under his armpit.

Honeypot accepted the tea absently and the envelope with much greater interest. She laid the prints on the table and spent some time studying them, laying her hands down so as to screen out all the figures except the part figure that interested her.

'I thought so,' she said. 'I bloody well thought so. I agree that they were hiding their faces deliberately. Your artist did a clever job but she had to make some guesses and some of those were wide of the mark. No wonder you got nothing positive. Let me take these away and I'll stand over an artist while he produces something better. But at the same time I'll see if I can't find some complete originals. I think I know exactly who these are. One of them, or maybe two, used to live next door to me. And believe me, they're a bad bunch. If I'm right – and I'll know by morning – this will turn out to be a far nastier business than you could possibly imagine.'

Luke exchanged a shrug of disappointment with Ian behind Honeypot's back. He was left to fold up and put away his email from Madeira.

★   ★   ★

She left them to wonder overnight. In the morning she returned with Ian and a box file of papers. She accepted a cup of tea and a seat on the terrace. Jane was walking Circe and Helena was in Edinburgh with Violet.

'It was several years ago now,' Honeypot told Luke. 'There was reason to believe that the occupier of the house next door to mine had something serious on his conscience. The superintendent heading my section asked me to look into it, which, I may say, he had no business to do while I was on maternity leave. To cut a long story very short, it turned out that Dr McGordon, my neighbour, was operating a racket along with his nephew Mr Samson, the surgeon. The world thought that they were some sort of saints, going abroad at their own expense and giving their services in deprived countries. They were going to deprived countries all right, ostensibly to give their services to medical clinics. In fact they were looking for living organ donors, desperate for money, who they could match to wealthy patients in this country. They would bring them here, do the transplant and send the donor back abroad. It was totally illegal but the most efficient way to transport organs and it served a very lucrative market in body parts

183

– a rich man in desperate need of an organ for himself or a loved one will pay whatever he's asked. Unfortunately for them, perhaps owing to a mistake by the theatre sister, they removed the good kidney from a man whose other kidney was diseased. Whether they knew at the time just what they were doing to him has never been decided. Bringing to Britain to act as a kidney donor a man who had only one good kidney raises all sorts of questions.

'Disaster was looming. There were no criminal charges, pending the outcome of a major lawsuit. Mrs McGordon had been packed abroad at the first hint of trouble. The passports of the two men had been seized. The men vanished and it was assumed that they had acquired other passports, but now it seems that they had changed identities and melted into the countryside. The disgraceful profits from their earlier ventures are salted away somewhere. They may not be doing themselves any favours, of course. The courts awarded the unfortunate farmer a sum large enough to keep him in dialysis for the rest of his life, and Scots law is adamant that when an award by a court isn't settled, a formidable rate of compound interest runs forever.

'As luck would have it, we already had their fingerprints and DNA on file from the time of their arrest and had gathered fresh ones from the house and the flat in Newton Lauder. They corresponded precisely. So not only are these really Dr McGordon and Mr Samson, no matter what they care to call themselves just now, but the woman who has been with them, who bears a superficial resemblance to the real Mrs McGordon, has been identified as one Judith Berellson. She is a well-qualified nurse and had been their partner in the illegal enterprise. She sometimes introduced the patient to them; sometimes she travelled with the donor and nursed both patient and donor after the operation. She was also the theatre sister who made the tragic mistake – if it really was a mistake. General opinion in the clinic where it all happened is that she is so evil and greedy a person that she could have made the mistake deliberately or at the least refrained from correcting the error. The recipient of the kidney was desperate and he is very rich. One other rumour,' Honeypot said disdainfully, 'is that she is said to be sexually voracious if not insatiable. Perhaps that's what she wanted the money for.

'Mr Fellowes here has been investigating

Yardstone House. A picture has been emerging. Those two men are, by repute, brilliant as doctors and could have made excellent livings at their professions; but some people are incapable of behaving honourably. They see themselves as superior beings and honest dealing as the prerogative of weaklings and losers. It seems clear that they have a new racket. They would call it a business but it's a racket sure enough. They took over the lease of Yardstone House and after minimal alterations and decoration they opened as a cancer clinic or, to be more accurate, I suppose you should call it a hospice. It specializes in patients whose cancers are incurable. But they seem to have had some remarkable results. You may recall that a cancer drug that was hailed as the magic bullet, under the name of Mortumour, was withdrawn when the National Institute for Clinical Excellence refused to license it, partly on grounds of cost but also because the side effects could be quite horrendous or even fatal.'

She nodded to Ian Fellowes who took up the story. 'It seems that Dr McGordon, in the name of Dr Ellis, the Yardstone House manager, had been advertising Mortumour on the Internet, not mentioning any side effects of course. Ellis seems to be a bumbling old fool who does whatever he's told to do. Patients already diagnosed with cancer and those who suspected that they might have it were soon knocking on his door at Yardstone. He took them into his care at a considerable weekly rate. He then had three sources of profit. There was the keep and nursing. Those who genuinely had cancer were nevertheless charged mightily for the injections of what they believed to be Mortumour. They died anyway. But those who only *thought* that they had it gave blood samples and were scanned. They were told that the diagnosis was confirmed. They would be given large and expensive doses of the fake Mortumour, concocted in the small room behind the office at Kempfield, and in some instances were operated on by the nephew, Mr Samson. Add to those results the fact that they managed to administer the Mortumour without any of the dreaded side effects and you can see that their reputation was escalating.'

Luke pursed his lips in a silent whistle. 'I knew that there were some ruthless people in the world,' he said, 'but this goes beyond belief.'

'Open your mind to it,' said Honeypot.

'This is real. And it isn't the end of it.'

'I'm not calling you a liar,' Luke said shakily. 'I'm just finding it difficult to believe that any educated Briton could be so evil, not impulsively and opportunistically but in a calculating way.'

Honeypot looked at him with tolerant amusement. 'That says much for your innocent mind and the sheltered life you've led. It's my experience that there's no deed so evil that you can be sure that nobody has ever done it. And age, race, gender or socio-economic grouping has no bearing whatever. Get used to the idea.' She opened her box file and produced photographs that, from the context, had clearly been taken by the police soon after arrests had been made. The expressions on the faces left Luke in no doubt that guilt and fury were evident. 'Are these not who we're talking about?'

Luke nodded. 'Definitely.'

Honeypot resumed, 'Now, let's move onward. What did you get from Madeira? It's written in English?'

Luke sighed. He suspected that she had chosen an unpropitious moment. He unfolded the printout from his pocket. 'They know better than to write to me in Portuguese. It's over Senhor Bustini's name although some secretary will have written the core of it. It begins with greetings...' It began, in fact, with a whole page of greetings. 'It goes on. *We have three possible groups for you to consider. None perfectly matched the pictures that you sent but you did warn us that there would be errors. The first is a couple only, two men, the older resembles the one in the picture the other less so. The second is three; they are rather like but they arrived here on Thursday the 15. Third is four, two men and two women. We can take photographs if you wish—*'

'For God's sake, no!' Honeypot exclaimed. 'Anybody following them around with a camera would scare them over the far horizon. Let me see that.'

Luke tried to hang on to the printout but Honeypot was determined and she had the weight of the law on her side. She triumphed in the brief tug-of-war and scanned the print rapidly. 'You old devil!' she snapped. 'The last part of this is an invitation to fly out at their expense and overhaul all their photographic publicity material, make sure that it's all up to date and replace any that was taken in less than ideal weather or before the garden was mature. He says that it's a perfect time for the flowers, the island's in full bloom and they'll pay everything.'

The two officers looked at Luke reproach-fully. 'And you told me that you'd used up all your favours,' Ian said.

'I don't think that I put it quite like that,' Luke said weakly.

'You're the only person who can go,' Honeypot pointed out. 'Nobody's going to authorize an expensive trip and several days' absence on the very speculative grounds that we've got so far. And I've seen a lot of your wildlife photography around. You're the one person I can think of with enough skill, patience and good reason for carry-ing a camera, to get photographs without alarming them. Even if they recognized you, you'd have a perfectly valid reason for being there. If we can get photographs identifying them as the fugitive doctors, we might be able to move against them with the aid of the Madeira police.'

'This is the very best time of year here,' Luke said. 'I don't want to miss any of it.'

Honeypot said, 'It's turning cold. Shall we move indoors?'

The sky had darkened and a chill breeze was blowing. Reluctantly, Luke led the way into his sitting room. The sky outside was so dark that he had to switch on the wall lights.

'Madeira will be gorgeous just now,'

Honey said as she lowered herself into one of the wing chairs.

'Too damn hot. And I can't get away. I have two great-granddaughters...'

'One of whom,' Ian said, 'spends all day hospital visiting and the other is quite old enough to look after herself.'

'I can't just run off and leave my business.'

'You were complaining to me about the boredom of retirement,' said Ian. Luke had the impression that he was trying not to laugh.

'Who'd look after the Kempfield Centre?'

Luke thought that he had the advantage but Ian answered a question with a question. 'How many other directors are there on the management committee?'

'Half of them wouldn't know a—'

'How many?'

'Well, eleven. But you can't expect me to leave a young girl to look after herself in an isolated place like this.'

'Take her with you,' Honeypot said.

'She doesn't have a passport.'

Honey looked at him coldly. 'Get the girl a BVP. Better still, let me have passport photographs of her and I'll fix it. I still have some clout.'

Luke turned his head to look out of the

191

window. The sky was solidly slate-grey and large drops of rain were blowing against the glass. There was a sudden flicker of lightning followed closely by a clap of thunder. It seemed that even the weather had turned against him. Somehow Madeira seemed less distant. 'I suppose so,' he said.

ELEVEN

The weather had suffered a relapse into the more usual British summer drizzle, giving Luke the motivation to go along with the decision that had already been thrust upon him. The prospect of a trip to Madeira also offered an easy solution to part of another problem. The school term had left serious teaching behind and had descended into a mixture of exams and tests with sporting challenges and almost anything calculated to keep the little devils off the streets and out of trouble. Jane and Violet, while showing to the world a picture of sisterly affection, were covertly at daggers drawn and, from previous experience, Luke was unhappily aware that a hissing, spitting, hair-pulling fight could erupt at any mention of Roddy's name. Jane's head teacher was easily persuaded that after the shock of her great adventure a period of rest in sunshine and flowers would do Jane a world of good.

Sr Bustini's reply to Luke's email had been that Jane would be very welcome to come along. Luke suspected that both visitors were being written off against tax.

Meanwhile, Honeypot continued to sweep all before her. Jane's passport appeared as if by magic. Luke wondered how anybody who looked so delicate and feminine, and who he had supposed to be without arrogance, could ride so roughshod over opposition. She made him think of a steamroller designed by a florist.

She briefed him thoroughly on what she wanted from him. 'You will be there to do three things,' she said sternly. 'One, find them if they're there and email me some photographs by which I can make a positive ID. Two, find out what they're up to. They won't be sitting on their hands. We're being very careful not to make any waves that could extend to Madeira, but we've found a disgruntled ex-member of staff. Dr McGordon had been hinting to certain patients, the better heeled ones without a lot of relatives in Britain, that he could arrange for them to end their days in the sunshine and flowers of some tropical or subtropical paradise. Anyone who, like myself, has a jaundiced view of the doctor might suspect that he does indeed intend them to end their days, but only after paying a fat fee for the treatment of a non-existent cancer and possibly also making a will in the doctor's favour, taking out an insurance policy and contributing certain valuable body parts to his unofficial organ bank.

'The most likely guess is that they may be looking for premises to start another clinic, if they haven't already done so. Find out if there are any British-owned clinics or nursing homes. Probably not. So far as we've been able to find out, only two or three patients have taken the doctors up on the offer of a sunshine deathbed and those seem to have disappeared completely. The offer only seems to have been made to those with no devoted relatives to ask nasty questions. In one instance, a forgotten great-niece showed up and wanted to visit her aged great-aunt and eventually received a letter from the great-aunt, typed, saying that she did not want to be bothered. The younger woman has been adamant that the wording is not what her great-aunt would have used, but she has been fobbed off and told that her elderly relative is now deceased. She is still trying to find out the burial site.'

Luke was becoming less and less happy about the proposed errand. 'If you're suggesting that elderly patients, with or without cancer, were transported abroad and disposed of, let me point out that I can't possibly go investigating possible murders in a foreign country.'

'There would be no point,' Honeypot said. 'I doubt very much if they'd be taken to Madeira for the purpose. Any warm place where they aren't too fussy about burials would suit. North Africa, perhaps. Have I shocked you?'

'Of course you have. This is the most shocking series of – what? – conjectures that I've ever heard.'

'I'm glad that you feel like that,' said Honeypot. She looked earnestly into his eyes and Luke had to make a special effort to take in what she was saying. 'It's what I hoped for. I want you to see that these people are bad through and through. I want you devoted to the cause of putting these people away.

'Your third task, help me to coax any or all of them to return to Britain where we can nab them without all the fuss, publicity and uncertainty of extradition.'

Luke was still unhappy. 'Are you really empowered to send civilians to do your dirty work abroad?' he asked.

She smiled charmingly. Her smile reached into his still active libido and raised a head of steam. 'Nobody's sending you anywhere. You're volunteering, as a good citizen, and don't you forget it. Now let's discuss the encryption of emails.'

After a flurry of activity the appointed day arrived, rushing at them all too soon. A traffic car whisked them to the boundary with the Strathclyde police area where a Strathclyde car took them over and delivered them to Glasgow Airport. Luke, who hated flying and detested tourist class, was relieved to find that instructions had been wired that they were to travel first class. Jane, who had never flown before, would cheerfully have travelled in the hold. She even took in her stride the very strict security and the implication that followers of Islam were awaiting their chance to blow the plane out of the sky. Even the loss of her favourite nail scissors failed to dampen her spirit. She had disregarded Luke's advice to put anything sharp into her case to go into the hold.

The four-hour trip passed in reasonable comfort. Luke was able to answer most of Jane's questions. Jane turned fretful, worrying about Circe. It had been agreed that Helena and Violet, between visiting Roddy McWilliam and all the chores necessary for survival, would not have time for the serious walking necessary for a young Labrador. Circe had been put in the care of a local keeper who undertook boarding and walking on the side.

'Will she be missing me?' Jane asked several times. It was a question to which either answer would be wrong and Luke avoided it by turning the subject. He was running out of subjects by the time small islands began to appear. Then Madeira itself, with the volcano lost in cloud.

There were still cranes around the airport. During the years that Luke had been visiting the island the airport had grown from what had been described as 'looking like somebody's garden path fallen off a cliff' and had been extended on piles out over the ocean. The whole complex was now much more spacious but there was still the same old turbulence over the shoreline as they came in to land.

José, a chauffeur who had driven Luke many times before, smoothed their paths through the formalities. José was showing his age but he carried their luggage and Luke's heavy camera case without apparent effort. They were transferred into a stretched and air-conditioned limousine that seemed to extend forever, without giving Jane much chance to notice the heat. When they were sliding effortlessly out into the motorway Jane asked, 'When José held the door for us, you said *"Obrigado"*. That means thank you, doesn't it?'

Luke was still recovering from the bumpy landing but he said that it did.

'Well, when I said it to him, he laughed. Why did he laugh, GG?'

'*"Obrigado"* just means obliged, a masculine adjective. It takes the gender of the person speaking, not the listener. You're a girl. You say *"Obrigada"*.'

Jane put her nose up. 'That's sexual discrimination,' she said. 'What else do you know in Madeiran?'

'Portuguese. They speak Portuguese. And

I've forgotten what little I ever knew. They nearly all speak English, the ones you're likely to come into contact with, but they appreciate it if they see that you've at least tried a little bit.'

'Will you buy me a Portuguese dictionary?'

'I'll buy you a phrasebook. Much more useful.'

They wound their way along the coastal road, past small clusters of buildings fitted in wherever there was space and a not too precipitous site. Jane was surprised but not dumbstruck by the flowers. 'GG, what's that tree?'

'Which tree?'

'The yellow one.'

'That's the golden trumpet tree. It's a little past its best.'

'And that one?'

'I don't know,' Luke said grumpily. He had missed his nap. Even in first class, the seat backs were not high enough to give headrest to anyone of his stature.

'GG, there's a book at home about Madeira with photographs of all the flowers and things and it says that you took the photographs.'

'That doesn't mean that I can remember

all their names now. That book's twenty years old.'

Jane was about to argue. But the Bay of Funchal had come into view and the motorway was skirting the back of Funchal with the help of some masterly engineering, soaring over deep valleys and plunging through tunnels. Luke, who had seen it all before, leaned his head back against the comfortable upholstery and dozed. Jane saved up her questions for later.

They quitted the motorway and filtered down towards the ocean to the flatter land where hotels, shops and restaurants were fitted together into every small but valuable space. The Bustini Grande had a larger site than most, allowing a garden, two tennis courts and three swimming pools. Luke woke up, refreshed, as the limo drew up at the impressive entrance. The hotel reared up for ten stories but the frontage was broken up into a parade of balconies, each edged with tumbling flowers.

Jane said, 'It's *hot!*'

'It's a little warm,' said her great-grandfather. 'That's all.'

José carried their bags to reception. Jane said *'Obrigada'*, which earned her another and larger smile. José told Luke the extension number to call whenever he needed transport and bowed himself out. A smart young receptionist asked whether they had a reservation, but when Luke gave his name she suddenly showed more than token respect. A suite had been reserved and when they were settled in Sr Bustini would be pleased if they would join him for dinner in the adjoining suite.

Jane said, *'Obrigada'* again. A porter appeared and carried their luggage across the marble floor, up in the American lift and to their suite along a richly carpeted corridor with few doors. Jane said *'Obrigada'* once more, but the porter's smile may have been mostly for the tip which, in such surroundings, Luke felt must not be less than generous.

Jane, who had lived for most of her short life in the Scottish Borders, was impressed by the opulence of their accommodation. She was delighted by the view over the shore and part of the Atlantic to the Desertas islands on the horizon; but she was trying hard to look as though such alien scenes were everyday matters. While Luke rested again and then took his time bathing and dressing in his best lightweight suit, she had showered quickly, demanded a few euros from Luke and set off, ostensibly in search of the promised phrasebook but in fact for a preliminary tour of the shops. There is little crime in Madeira. Luke reminded her to keep a grip on her purse, to use the pedestrian crossings and to watch for traffic coming from the left.

'You'd better know,' he said, 'that the Portuguese for how much is this? is "*Quanto custa?*"'

She pointed a finger at him. 'So you do know some Portuguese!'

He shrugged. 'I was tired. I didn't feel like trying to remember.'

Jane nodded. It was a perfectly satisfactory explanation. 'I can remember that. *Quanto custa?* How much cost?'

Luke treated himself to another nap. He had shaved with care and made himself presentable before Jane returned in triumph, bringing with her the phrasebook and apparently having already mastered some of its contents but in need of help with the pronunciation. She had also purchased some aftershave for Luke, a floral perfume for herself and some totally unsuitable costume earrings. 'It seems that I am now a senhorita,' she said.

'Don't let it go to your head. You always were. It just sounds better in Portuguese.'

'More glamorous,' she agreed. The heat of the day had almost passed but she was unaccustomed to the warmth and humidity. Luke considered her moistness unladylike. He chivvied her to take a quick shower and make ready.

'Did you take your pills?' Jane demanded. She felt that she had taken over Helena's position as a quasi-mother.

'I'll take them now.'

Jane nodded. When she returned, fresh and delectable, she inspected his pill dispenser and was satisfied.

Luke had no great fondness for the Madeiran wines, which he found a little heavy for his taste. He was sipping a gin and tonic from the minibar and Jane, now cooler, more crisply dressed and feeling like a proper grown-up lady, was finishing a maracuja, when there was a tap on the door. No less a personage than the English assistant head waiter announced that Sr Bustini was awaiting them.

In the corridor, Jane whispered, 'How do I say hullo?'

'Say *Boa tarde*. That's good afternoon, but it counts as early evening. You'll find that they both speak very good English.'

The adjoining suite was even more luxurious but showed signs of being permanently occupied. Luke recalled hearing, after his last previous visit, that Sr and Sra Bustini had decided to make this their permanent base and had moved their entire office on to the floor below. From there, all functions of the Bustini empire were monitored. The couple was now waiting in a sitting room furnished with deep carpets and plump easy chairs. The carpet and curtains were thick, adding to the impression of luxury, even if the colours were rather bright for British taste.

Luke had first met Sr Bustini (as he was now known) more than a half-century earlier. At that time, Senhor Bustini's male secretary had had the temerity to inseminate the boss's only daughter. The wrath of the wronged father was immense. Luke had used his powers of persuasion to arrange a wedding instead of a hired hit man. His efforts had brought about a reconciliation. But that tale has already been told. What was at the time a comparatively modest empire in hotels and leisure had passed to the daughter who still occupied the chair with her husband, who had changed his name to hers, as managing director.

Business, the production of brochure and poster photographs of the prestigious buildings, had brought them together again every few years and, each time, Luke had been shocked to see how his old friend was ageing. He supposed that Bustini for his part had been as surprised by the damage that the years had inflicted on Luke. But this time his grounds for concern were more tangible. Francisco Bustini rolled himself across the floor in a wheelchair to greet him.

Luke's concern must have shown. They shook hands and Francisco smiled, showing very white teeth. 'Do not worry, old friend,' he said. 'I am not yet crippled. The penalty of eternally searching to find the very best chefs in the world is that one must sample their work. An enjoyable occupation but age and weight together are not kind to the knees. And this must be the famous Jane?'

Jane blushed but she remembered to say *'Boa tarde,'* with a fair imitation of Luke's accent but with her surprise showing.

Senhora Bustini was also smiling. She shook hands graciously. 'But of course we know of your adventure,' she said. 'We have the British satellite television in all the rooms and as soon as the staff saw my husband's old friend in the picture they telephoned up here. We were in time to hear the whole story. You were very brave. You must be in love with the boy, to venture so far and headfirst down a narrow well for his sake. Am I not right?' she asked Luke.

Jane's blush turned scarlet.

'She is very young,' Luke said.

'A woman is never too young!' Senhora Bustini said indignantly. Luke thought that she should know. She had never been beautiful but the ageing process, so often cruel, had toned down her earlier ugliness into acceptable plainness tempered by an expression of benevolence and an afterglow of sensuality. In a beauty contest for the elderly, she might well have made it into the upper third.

Luke knew better than to enter into an argument about love with a woman, especially one whose race was of Latin extraction. 'You could be right,' he said. 'Jane has certainly been showing all the signs for the last year or more.'

Jane's blush became incandescent and she contrived a series of gestures and facial distortions designed to convey to her ancestor that that line of discussion was not appreciated, but at least she was silenced and abashed. Her elders were thus granted peace to enjoy a pre-dinner drink and an excellent meal served in the adjacent dining room by the assistant head waiter. Luke pleaded recurrent gout and was permitted to drink water. News and opinions were exchanged. Sr Bustini outlined the photographs that were needed. The subject of fugitive doctors was avoided until coffee had been served in the sitting room. A signal must have passed, because three men filed into the room. Their ages seemed to range between forty and fifty and each bore a strong resemblance to Sr Bustini. 'My sons,' he confirmed. 'Luis, Christopher and Arturo.' At a nod from their father, the three men shook hands punctiliously and then seated themselves in a row on a settee. Each was groomed to the standard to be expected in the higher echelons of the hotel business. Each had their father's proud chin and more than a trace of the looks that, around fifty years earlier, had captivated the heiress to the hotel combine that her father was building into an empire. Neither had had any cause to regret what had been something of a shotgun union.

The senhora excused herself. Apparently this was man's business.

'Each of them manages a hotel here on Madeira,' said Francisco Bustini. 'I also have four granddaughters. They are in training and in the fullness of time they will enter the business. They are here on Madeira where I can keep an eye on them, as you say, but they are employed at other hotels in different ownership.' He smiled with satisfaction. 'In that way they will bring back understanding of how others organize their businesses.

'I have explained your ... your problem to my sons, but you need not look at me like that, old friend. I have ... emphasized, is that right?' He was looking at Jane, who nodded eagerly. 'I have emphasized,' he resumed, 'that the matter is very confidential. They may consult anyone who they might trust with their life and fortune, but the pictures that you sent me are not to leave their hands.'

Luke said, 'This last is important. It is not only that if they get wind of anyone enquiring into where they are they will vanish away as they have done twice already. It is also that they have already killed and I am sure that the young man who my great-granddaughter pulled out of the well was intended to died down there. We do not want anyone else to die. Nobody must be seen or heard to be watching them or asking questions.'

There was solemn nodding. Luke thought that they were taking the warning seriously. Whether they could convince others to be as cautious might be another matter.

Francisco Bustini let a moment pass in silence in order to let the vital nature of the warning sink in. Then he said, 'Between us, we have access to staff in eight hotels, the best hotels on Madeira. I exclude Reid's, but I doubt if even your criminals could or would aspire to a hotel with seven stars. I am hoping that our newest one, under construction in Singapore – but that is another matter. I have no doubt that my granddaughters by now have suitors who hope to better themselves by marrying into my dynasty. They will not be employees of the same hotels – courtship between couples employed in the same hotel is discouraged.' His face pinched into an expression of disapproval.

Momentarily Luke felt offended at the presumption of using the word *dynasty*. Self-aggrandizement is not in the British nature. But he reconsidered. His old friend was founding a dynasty indeed. He had continued the work of his father-in-law, building up a chain of quality hotels and maintaining a standard exceeded only by Reidand its very few competitors. That would mean, give or take a lover or two, a round dozen of employees in that number of the better hotels, each of whom would have valuable contacts.

They seemed to be waiting for him to open the bowling. Very well. 'Let me begin,' he said, 'by assuring you again, if you're in any doubt, that these are very bad people. And they are very cautious. If we involve your police at this stage, they will know and they will be gone. They are very shy about being photographed, which is why the pictures you have been given are composites. I am helping the police back in Britain. They want to know where these people are, under what names, and what they are up to. Unless you can accept my word for this we may as well stop now.'

Francisco Bustini drew himself up. 'I accept Mr Grant's assurance,' he said. 'I have known him since before any of you was born. He would only tell the truth.'

There was a silence. The men looked at each other. Luke's heart sank. This was not going to work.

Arturo waited politely until it was clear that his elders were silent. Alone among the Bustini menfolk he sported a small beard, kept short and very tidy. He spoke hesitantly. 'It is clear that these people have not stayed in any hotel where we have friends. They may be in a ... a self-catering apartment. But perhaps I can offer a place to begin. My daughter Raffaella is walking out with the manager of a car hire firm. He has an interest in the firm, so it will be a good match although it is early days yet for talking about marriage.'

Signor Bustini frowned. 'Yes, yes. It will be an excellent match, but your daughter's prospects are not what we are here to discuss.'

'Your pardon. Under a vow of secrecy, she showed him your pictures. A man who looks much like the older man in your picture hired a small silver Seat three days ago. The address given was care of a bank. I have the details here.'

'Excellent!' Francisco Bustini slapped his knee. 'Let our friends know to keep on watching, but give them the details of the car. We wish to know all of its comings and goings. And ... We have no information from that bank?' Heads were shaken.

Luis, he whose very germination triggered an important turn in Luke's life, had a question. 'Do we know what class of accommodation they are most likely to use?'

Luke found himself in some difficulty. 'I have never known them personally,' he said. 'But the older man lived at one time next door to the officer leading this enquiry. I can send an email to ask that very question. I believe that they will not be short of money but will be spending it with care. And they will not wish to be too visible – you know what I mean?'

His old friend grinned. 'We have the same word in Portuguese.'

'Then you will understand. Perhaps a small, discreet hotel with a weekly or monthly rate or, as you say, a self-catering apartment...'

'This you can leave with us.'

'I do so with every confidence.'

Luke had rather expected Francisco's three sons to hurry away to make a start on their enquiries. He had forgotten the advantages of modern technology. For a few minutes there was rapid murmuring in Portuguese into top-of-the-range mobile phones. When word had been spread and the sons were free to join their father in a drink, Jane found herself the centre of an admiring group. With becoming modesty she answered questions about her tracking and rescue of Roddy McWilliam. She made much use of her few words of Portuguese and of her Portuguese dictionary. Furnishing the missing words and correcting her pronunciation became a friendly game, flavoured with innocent flirtation, among her new admirers.

Luke and Francisco, feeling rather left out of the admiration society, talked to each other.

TWELVE

The Bustini chain of hotels on Madeira included three older and smaller establishments and four with five-stars. There were about a dozen others, scattered around the temperate world wherever the far-seeing management could anticipate an influx of well-heeled tourists.

The photographs of the smaller Madeiran hotels had been taken by an unambitious

213

local photographer, competently but without flair. The larger and more recent hotels had been considered worthy of the expense of bringing Luke out, but even these shots had now dated. Extensions had been built, pools added. Trees had grown, blown down or died natural deaths and been replaced by different species. Travel agents producing brochures of holidays at the uppermost end of the market want all details to be up to date, including photographs. Francisco Bustini could see his chance of killing a whole flock of birds with a single stone – doing a favour for the old friend who he still credited with triggering his own good fortune, at the same time updating the photography of all the Madeiran hotels of the chain and only having to fly Luke to and fro the once. As a bonus he would also be refreshing the sense of obligation that maintained Luke's willingness to act as his agent in Britain during emergencies of the overbooking or flight cancellation kind. That service alone, in dealing with travel agents and airlines when trouble occurred, was worth more than Luke ever cost him so that when Luke suggested that Francisco's family and employees might be expecting some reward for their present help Francisco had waved the matter aside.

Luke, who had plenty to do at home, would have fretted if left to his own devices and at the mercy of Jane's eternal thirst for knowledge; but Francisco had given him a free hand to update and improve the brochure and poster photographs and had lent him José. The stretched limo, Francisco's personal transport, would have been included except that Luke preferred something less conspicuous. A small Mercedes had been substituted. They made a good team. José knew every short cut and every diversion. Luke's knowledge of the geography was sufficient that he knew exactly at what time of day the sun would be placed to perfection for each hotel and its garden. Sometimes Jane came along and made herself useful, holding reflectors or branches of blossom. She even showed some promise as a photographer of the future. Just as often she remained in the hotel, practising her burgeoning fluency in Portuguese on maids and waiters. On the afternoon of the second full day, she was left at the hotel.

Luke had acquired his mobile phone second-hand when his previous phone drowned in the canal at the bottom of the hill at home. The previous owner, who was rather a genius with electronics, had caused the ringing tone to be replaced by a girl's voice calling 'I'm ready' in a very suggestive tone. Luke had retained it because it appealed to his sense of humour and made a talking point; but that advantage was offset by the fact that it was only too easily ignored when Luke was in a crowd. The call came just as Luke had composed the shot that he wanted, showing the Bustini Imperial Hotel from its best angle and avoiding the gap left where two palm trees had blown down. The gardens were at their best with a tulip tree and two beautiful Australian flame trees in full flower. Purple and red bougainvillaea dripped from troughs edging the balconies.

At a table behind him a group was polishing off their second bottle of malmsey and out-talking each other. José glanced towards the swimmers in the nearby pool but Luke knew where the voice came from. He also knew from bitter experience, however, that although the flowers would be there tomorrow the photograph might not. If you let the perfect shot go by, the gods will punish you. The weather will have moved on or, as in one instance, the washing up of a dead whale had put an expression of disgust on to the faces of everyone within shot. He finished composing the shot, waited until a girl with an unsuitably coloured bikini had moved out of frame and a swimmer had moved into the perfect position to fill a gap in his composition. He took his photograph, repeated it just in case and took out his phone.

The senior of Francisco's four secretaries, a plump lady with a jolly laugh, was on the line. Her English was good but careful. 'We have received a call from a friend of Mr Christopher. He is concierge at the Atlas Grande. He says that the two men in your pictures had a lunch beside the pool. He was not sure that they were they –' her voice hesitated but went on '– but he watch them to their motorcar and see them drove off towards Ribeira Brava. It was the car.'

'How long ago was this?' Luke asked.

'Not long. Perhaps fifteen minutes.'

Luke thanked her, closed the call and began a hurried gathering up of his photographic gear. 'Get the car, José.'

On the *need to know* principle, José had not been told of the prime reason for Luke's visit. As soon as they were in the car, Luke directed their route out of Funchal on the coast road towards Ribeira Brava. As the hotels, restaurants and shops gave way to open country and banana plantations, he explained the immediate mission, laying great emphasis on the evil nature of his quarry and the overriding need to avoid alarming them. José nursed the car through the afternoon traffic while Luke tried to look everywhere at once –at number plates, at parked cars, at pedestrians. But it was hopeless. There were too many minor side streets and hidden places behind business premises where workers or those in the know could park a vehicle. Outside Funchal it was worse. The hillside behind the banana plantations, mostly rocky and barren, was ribbed by former lava-flows and water-courses, now sheltering scattered orchards, farms and hamlets. They drove on anyway. It was the least unpromising option.

About five kilometres outside Funchal they passed Camara de Lobos ... Another five and they were nearing Ribeira Brava. From there the road continued along the coast. They were granted a sight of it and of a half-dozen cars waiting patiently while several machines attended to a road slip. None of the cars was small and silver. But another road branched off, to struggle up the mountainside and join a hair-raising road down to the north coast, the only road to cross the waist of the island. The Mercedes would have the legs of a small Seat with two men aboard. They turned to the hill.

The road was surprisingly good but they came up behind a heavy vehicle that they were forced to follow to Serra de Agua. At that point the road was broken by several junctions. Luke could not imagine his quarry living so far from the hub of activity but they parked the Mercedes and he sent José to enquire at a house. There was no word of two or three strangers renting a house or lodgings in the area. They turned and made a dispirited return to the coast road and Funchal.

That evening, Luke wrote an email to Honeypot:

Their car has been seen but word did not reach me until too late to follow up. We know the general area into which they were heading and can only hope that they were going home.

And to Helena:

Jane is learning Portuguese at a speed that I would not have believed possible. She is being very helpful and well behaved. Long may it last.

When he opened his email connection to send his two emails, another incoming message, from Helena, came up;

Roddy has been recovering well except that his memory still stops at the point when he was about to leave Kempfield. He can get out of bed on his own and hobble around without assistance. This would be a cause for celebration except for one factor. His mother was careless in walking through the car park in front of the hotel and a reversing van knocked her down. Not too serious, but she has to stay in hospital for a few days until they can be sure that her ankle is mending properly. She was quite frantic about Roddy though I thought, and he was sure that he could manage quite well on his own.

I said that he could stay with us. After all, we have plenty of beds until you get back. But this morning I went up with his breakfast and was not too pleased with the scene I intruded on. There was a lot of what I think the Americans call 'heavy petting' going on – not quite having sex but only a quick fumble away from it. God knows neither of us is

*exactly prudish and Violet must know by
now that we share a bed.*

This news drove the two doctors out of
Luke's mind for the moment. As a great-
grandfather who had been landed with
responsibility for two great-granddaughters,
he had made sure that they knew the bio-
logical facts and had ready sources of
information about more delicate aspects of
sex. He had dreaded the day when more
immediate intervention might be required
but it seemed that the day had arrived. He
was torn between an ancestor's anxiety, a
memory of the delights of young love and a
vicarious pride that his grandson's daughter
could wreak havoc in the male sex. He
replied:

*Tell her that sex is not for a weekend, it
should be forever. Unless you feel confident –
and you have more chance of getting it right
than I have because you, after all, have been
a girl – try to stall until you can send Roddy
home or I return. Or, of course, until his
mother comes out of hospital. She may have
the answer. We do have a tradition of early
marriage in my family but I do not yet feel
ready to be a great-great-grandfather.*

While on the subject, you and I are not, as you hint, setting a good example. Perhaps it is time that we regularized our situation. I'm sure that Hannah, my late wife, would understand that I have remained single, and therefore in a sense faithful to her memory, for more than fifty years. An email is not the ideal way to suggest marriage, but even if we wait until I can go down on one knee I might not be able to get up again without your help, which would be less than romantic. Think it over.

That night, when he went to give Jane the goodnight kiss that she still expected, he found her on her balcony, looking over the lights of Funchal. She looked up at him and said, 'I opened the Internet in the laptop, to see if there were any messages for me. Can I be a bridesmaid?'

'She hasn't said that she'll marry me.'

'Of course she will,' Jane said firmly. 'It's what she's always wanted. But don't let Roddy and Violet rush into marriage. She's much too young, never mind what she's been getting up to.'

'She's older than you are,' Luke retorted. 'Much. And you're not supposed to know about these things.'

She lowered her voice. At night, conversations could be heard from balcony to balcony. 'I know some and what I don't know I can puzzle out.'

Luke would have let the exchange go at face value except for the remarks that had passed at the press conference. He thought urgently. 'When you're Vi's age, if Roddy comes to me and asks for your hand in marriage, will you still be too young?'

'No. But I'm already more mature than she is.'

That was probably true but it did little for his peace of mind. It occurred to him that he was unlikely to be still around when Jane reached Violet's age. For once, the thought was rather comforting.

Rather than be plagued with a thousand questions that, taken out of context, would take ten times longer than the asking time to answer, Luke had kept Jane up to date on how the search was progressing. She had even made some helpful suggestions. Over breakfast she asked him, 'Where are you going today?'

Luke had slept badly, plagued by dreams in which Jane was an old lady but apparently still setting her cap at Roddy while

Violet seemed to have regressed to baby-hood. It took him a moment to recover the decision that he had made the previous evening. 'I'm going back over the track that José and I took yesterday,' he said at last. 'I want to make sure that we didn't miss anything. Also, there's a small hotel I still have to photograph.'

'Can I come along? Learning Portuguese is getting to be a bit of a drag.'

Luke smiled and ruffled her hair. 'Of course you can come. I'll be glad of a pair of sharp young eyes with me. And I've been surprised at how you could keep your head down over your books for so long at a time.'

'It's not so bad when you can help yourself to learn by having conversations with people about what's going on.'

'I'm sure that's true. And it's the best way to learn.'

Before they drove off, Luke checked his emails. There was one from Helena:

This is one of your better ideas. We can talk details when you come home. Meantime consider yourself an engaged man and behave accordingly.

I have had a panic message from Charlie at Kempfield. The grey paint that they use on furniture etc that's going to be painted is running out. Where do they go to for more?

He replied:

Morrison the painting contractor saves us all his partly used cans. Mix all the colours together and you get that battleship grey. I suspect that that's why the Admiralty always uses it. Tell Charlie to speak to Abe Morrison.

The Hotel Frangipani was close to their route out of Funchal, on a narrow old street shadowed by flowering trees. The heavily modelled frontage only saw the sun in the mornings so they called there on their way out of town. A thin layer of cloud was softening the harsh light to perfection. Within a few minutes Luke had done all that he could do for the morning. The equally sculptured rear of the building would have to wait for an afternoon visit.

They had stowed the cameras and the light-reflecting umbrella in the car and were about to move off when Luke's phone made its suggestive noise. Luke listened for a minute and then disconnected. 'That call was from Atlas Grande,' he said. 'The Seat was in their basement garage but the duty receptionist is certain that nobody with those names or descriptions is registered in the hotel. It seems likely that they were doing some shopping in the supermarket next door. They've gone now.'

'Never mind,' said Jane, 'They'll be back. We could have lunch there and wait for them.'

Her great-grandfather shook his head. 'They won't be back. 'They took tea in the restaurant and the older man – Dr Mc-Gordon – had a row with the head waiter about the quality of the tea. He insisted that the water wasn't boiling. Much though it grieves me to side with the enemy, he was probably right. Knowing that we're interested and that there might be the offer of a reward or a better job from Francisco, she told the waiter to listen to what was said but his English isn't good and from what he could gather they were talking a lot about the quality of the tea.' He was still nursing his mobile phone. 'I'll give Francisco a call and see if he can't get somebody to coax a little more out of that waiter. While that's going on, we could revert to Plan A and repeat yesterday's safari.'

★ ★ ★

Luke directed José out of Funchal by way of lesser streets where a small, silver Seat might be tucked away in the many nooks and forecourts. But there was none to be seen and they were soon back on the Estrada Monumental. With three or four diversions to explore minor dead ends that were similarly devoid of Seats, they covered the same route as before.

The same roadworks were causing the same bottleneck at Ribeira Brava. As they approached, a small group of waiting cars was allowed through towards them. Among them was a small, silver car that Luke thought was a Seat. He began to direct José to turn in pursuit but Jane said, 'Don't bother. Wrong number plate.'

'For once, I'm glad I brought you,' Luke said.

Jane accepted his comment in the spirit in which it was made. She laughed. 'You wanted sharp young eyes and that's what you got.'

'That's for sure. And I'm duly grateful.'

The Mercedes again made light work of the six kilometres up to the crest. For once there was no cloud and the views were breathtaking but they had still not seen the car that they were after. They were setting off on the return journey when Luke's phone made its suggestive noise.

Luke listened for a minute. When he put the phone away he told Jane, 'That was Francisco. If we speak to the head waiter at the Atlas Grande he may have something for us. José, back where we came from.'

In the hall of the Atlas Grande Hotel there was a noticeboard spelling out the times during which each meal would be served, but Luke knew that as long as there was a hungry guest seeking food he would be served. The tips were better if the guest thought that he was getting a special privilege.

The receptionist became quite animated when they entered but was apologetic. The head waiter was unavailable for the moment. If they would care to wait...

'Could we still get lunch?' Luke asked.

'But certainly.' She picked up the phone. Luke went out to speak to José who, as always, flatly refused to eat with his passengers but invariably brought sandwiches, which he ate in the shade of the car.

The dining room was emptying. The assistant head waiter allowed them to choose a table tucked against the window in a far corner of the room, where they would be behind a fat column and so granted a fair degree of privacy. Luke sat with his back to the column while Jane faced into the room. Their food came quickly. Luke could only pick at an omelette but Jane fell upon the dish that he recommended, which turned out to be a sort of paella of chicken mixed with seafood. She ate ravenously, which was as well because her meal was interrupted. When her plate was almost empty she suddenly dropped her cutlery and leaned forward.

'GG,' she whispered, 'they've just come in. They're being shown to a table just the other side of this pillar.'

Luke froze. He looked carefully around, moving only his eyes. As a photographer, he was well aware of how much can be revealed by reflections in glass. He soon found his own reflection in the one window that held it. The sunlight was catching only his hands and one shoulder. He leaned back. But when he picked up the reflection of the others he saw that all three were present. He decided that, contrary to his earlier impression that the fates were having fun tormenting him, they were now rolling the dice in his favour.

At first he could hear nothing. Then a party of noisy women got up and took their noisy chatter outside. The dining room became hushed. The trio at the other table were speaking softly but he found that he could hear most of what they said. The older man's voice finished an unintelligible sentence and then the woman spoke. 'I'll take the shopping back to the flat before the frozen stuff and the ice cream thaws out. Order that swordfish thing for me and I'll be back by the time it comes.'

The man's voice grunted agreement. 'Here is the car key,' he said.

Luke leaned forward and muttered urgently to Jane. 'I can't let them see me. Get out and find José. Follow her up and come back.'

Jane nodded and rose. The waiter was at her side immediately. *'Obrigada,'* she said. Her accent was much improved. *'Por favor, a conta,'* she added.

She walked out. The talk at the other table did not hesitate. Luke concluded that the quarry had never seen her with her great-grandfather and either did not understand Portuguese or accepted that a young girl might call for the bill. As the light tap of Jane's footsteps left the room the woman got up and followed with a heavier tread.

The waiter was approaching Luke but was waved away.

There ensued for Luke a period of the most abysmal frustration. Voices and the clatter of cutlery confused the sound that reached ears already long past their peak of efficiency. The gaps occurred whenever he was sure that they were coming to the subjects in which he was interested. He saw the Mercedes return and take up a parking place. The Seat remained out of his sight but he heard the woman return to her place and start work on her portion of swordfish. Between bites, she kept dragging the conversation back to subjects that she found more interesting. Her companions were bored but Luke was almost frantic. Jane had more sense than to risk everything by coming to join him. The head waiter approached but he had to shake his head at him.

But all such periods must end some time. There was a scraping back of chairs. A voice assured the head waiter that they would take their post-prandial tea back at their apartment rather than risk facing a brew made with less than ebullient water.

Luke decided not to follow them again. Instead, he got hold of the head waiter, who was eager to unburden himself. He had indeed questioned the waitress who had served the trio earlier.

'She heard comparatively little,' Luke told Jane as the Mercedes left the hotel, heading for the group of apartments where the woman had taken the frozen shopping. 'And she understood less. But she did remember one or two place names. Some of them, the head waiter assured me, were the names of shops. The only other name she remembered was Machico, but that's away the other side of Funchal, isn't it José?'

'Yes, Senhor.'

Jane found her voice. It came out as a squeak. 'Stop! GG, did you say Machico?'

José let the car roll a little further down the hill to where a splash of shade lay across the road.

'I did,' said Luke. 'Like I said, Machico's miles away on the other side of Funchal. In fact, it's just beyond the airport. But she thought that they agreed that Machico was as good as they could do.'

'A little up the hill from Ribeira Brava,' Jane said, 'there's a house set back from this road. You can only see the roof but it looks large. The name on the gatepost was Casa

Machico. Beside the gate there was a sign saying something about *venda*. I think that means For Sale.'

'Does it, by golly?' Luke exclaimed.

'Yes. I've been doing French at school and some of the words are the same. And there was a name under it with the word *advogado*. I think that must mean lawyer.'

'It sounds as if it might. Stop us when we get to the place. I want the name of that lawyer. Drive on, José. Back to Ribcira Brava.'

THIRTEEN

It often happens that while those concerned have no positive direction for their energy, all proceeds in an orderly manner. But as soon as truth begins to emerge shyly like Venus from the foam everybody feels a compulsion to become hyperactive on their own little piece of the overall endeavour. There was activity for the rest of that day, much of it wasted. By late the following morning, a clearer picture was emerging as to who was in overall charge, what the objectives might be and in what order of priority.

Luke had exchanged emails with Honeypot, receiving in reply to his report a lengthy reply including the following:

This would be an impossible time to request extradition. (Later Luke learned that at that very time the Portuguese were pressing for extradition of a woman suspected of poisoning her husband. The request was being refused due to inconsistencies in the evidence pointed out by British pharmacological experts, inconsistencies that were hotly denied by their opposite numbers.) *That being so, the precise residence of our three remains an interesting acquisition but for the moment of less importance. What we need is something to lure them back into Britain.*

Consultation with bankers suggests that, on the basis of our present knowledge, there is no prospect of tempting them back to Britain by some threat to their money. They are still clients of the solicitor Enterkin. His loyalty to his clients is well known. Any approach to him aimed at the passing of a false message would be communicated to them immediately.

Your discovery of their interest in Casa Machico opens another door. It does seem, as you say, that the two men paused at the Atlas Grande Hotel for a brief refreshment while they debated whether Casa Machico is the property that interests them. Find out as much as you can. Speed is essential; they may be considering some alternative building.

When he opened this email, Luke was seriously frustrated by the presence of his great-granddaughter in the room. The English language is not well provided with swear-words. Satisfactory relief to the feelings is most often obtained by imaginative word pictures produced by permutations on the few words that do exist. But Jane was already ahead of her classmates in the use of language and he had no intention of furthering her education in that regard. He uttered a wordless exclamation expressive of disgust.

Jane looked up anxiously. 'What's wrong, GG? Nothing at home?'

'Nothing like that,' Luke said. 'As far as I know, everybody's well. The object of your affection continues to make excellent progress.' (Luke had had enough of limiting himself to Basic English for the benefit of his Madeiran helpers.) 'It's just that damned policewoman. The detective inspector.'

'Honeypot? She told me I could call her that,' Jane added quickly.

Luke grunted. 'Call her what you like, with my blessing. I – we – gave her an excellent lead to where the people who attacked Roddy could be found. A word of thanks would not have been out of place. Even congratulations would be in order. But what do we get? Because some idiots in the Foreign Office or somewhere have refused to co-operate with the Portuguese legal system, she wouldn't be able to do anything through what she calls *the proper channels*. So she wants us to go on looking for them and find out everything they're doing so that she can decoy them back home. That would be unpaid, of course.'

Jane was about to share his indignation when she realized what suffering was actually entailed. 'So we have to stay out here with all this beastly sunshine and the horrible flowers and the hideously ugly women in bikinis,' Jane said. 'Well, poor you! It must be hell.'

Luke refused to smile despite the provocation. 'That's all very well, but it comes just when I want to get home and sort things out between me and Helena.'

'And between Vi and Roddy?' Jane asked

keenly.

'Have you been reading my emails?'

Jane seemed surprised. 'Yes, of course I have. You let me use your laptop to swap emails with the family and to look on the Internet for the explanations for things. I couldn't do any of that without seeing incoming messages.'

Jane sounded reasonable. Luke thought that there must be flaws in her argument. But even if it were possible for her to send and receive emails without opening the other messages he could not expect a young girl to ignore the brief but tantalizing summaries that appeared in the in-tray. Jane's intelligence had matured amazingly during the past year and, as might be expected of any young girl, she was much better versed in computers and the Internet than her great-grandfather. He decided against bandying arguments with her. She would probably win. 'So you know that something's going on between Vi and Roddy.'

'I knew that a long time ago.' Jane's voice sounded choked.

Luke moved to take a seat beside her on the couch. 'I'm sorry,' he said gently. 'I know that you have a crush on Roddy yourself. Well, I can't help you there and anyway

237

you're too young to be thinking about Roddy.'

Jane lifted her pert nose and sniffed. 'Don't say *crush*, GG. It makes me sound like some teenybopper mooning over her maths teacher or a spotty pop star. Shakespeare's Juliet was younger than I am. And I won't always be too young.' She was blinking back tears but her mouth was firm. 'GG, if Roddy and Vi asked you for permission to get married, what would you say?'

Luke had to think about that. Events seemed to be rushing at him. He no longer saw his own future stretching far ahead. To see Violet settled in a lasting relationship was a temptation. On the other hand...'I would suggest that they wait,' he said slowly. 'They're at an age when loyalties can be quickly formed and as quickly broken. I'd suggest that they waited two or three years, until Roddy's established in a career, and Vi too if that's what she wants. Or until I pop my clogs, whichever comes sooner.'

'Don't talk like that,' Jane said. 'We all know that you're going to live forever. You've said so yourself. That's good, what you said about Vi. She can keep him warm for me. I'll know when it's the right time to take over.' She tapped him on the chest.

'But that's just our secret, you understand. You mustn't tell Vi.' She kissed his cheek and skipped out of the room, leaving her great-grandfather with his jaw dropped. After a long life enriched by many affairs, he thought that he knew something about women. But sometimes it took his own great-granddaughters to convince him that he knew nothing. What on earth did they teach them in their magazines these days?

That evening, he spared a little time to curse the bad luck that had delivered him into Honeypot's clutches; but having been landed with the status of her agent in the war against evil, he was blessing the combination of chance and inspiration that had brought him once again to Francisco Bustini. The hotel industry is a huge boiling-pot. Rivalries keep factions apart but common interest draws them together and the more gregarious staff members soon get to know others of their calling. Luke could, of course, tell Honeypot to leave him in peace but he knew that he would not. His anger at the ruthless machinations that had so nearly brought disaster into his family was consuming. And, if challenged, he would have had to admit that he was being drawn on by the thrill of pursuit.

He phoned Francisco Bustini and asked for a discussion.

Francisco was very much in charge of the meeting but he had handed over the floor for the moment. Christopher was reporting. He said, 'The lawyer – Senhor Panzar – is said to be as honest as any lawyer ever is. I sent one of the busboys to leave an unimportant message for a client and to keep his eyes and ears open. While the secretary was busy finding out that the client had died a month ago, he looked around. He saw something of interest. A young girl fetched a file and went back into the partner's room. He was sure that he had seen her before and in a little while he remembered. She had been in the company of a friend of his who is an under-gardener where she used to work, at the Bustoni Grand.'

Francisco exchanged a look with Luke. 'So, we have an employee of the advocate, and this employee walks out with one of our employees. It seems that luck is running our way at last. This busboy, is he due for promotion?'

'I'll check,' said Christopher.

For a moment Luke recognized in Francisco's face traces of the guile that had won him his place near the pinnacle of the hotel hierarchy in Madeira. 'Do so. If he's ready and keen to be a table waiter, and if it would not make bad blood among the other busboys, suggest to him that his promotion might happen more speedily if he could persuade his young lady to obtain answers to one or two questions which Mr Grant will describe. Discover if there is a question of marriage. We might be able to offer a honeymoon package – in the off season naturally.'

'Of course,' said Christopher. A double room at the height of the season is worth real money. An empty room is worth nothing.

Some delicate negotiations must have been set in train. Luke had time to complete his photography on Francisco's behalf and was itching to get home and process the images. It was three days before another meeting was convened in Francisco's sitting room. Present were Francisco, Christopher, Luke, Jane and a dark and thin young man named Carlos. Luke thought that Carlos might be attractive to women, an opinion that was confirmed by Jane's suddenly modest countenance and soft voice – of which symptoms

Luke thought that Jane herself was unaware. Carlos remained standing throughout. His English was as good as that of all the other serving staff.

'Things are proceeding well,' Christopher said. 'It would seem that Carlos's fiancée, as she is now, was impressed by the reward that we offered. She has already chosen the hotel and is choosing dates. For her part of the bargain, she has already looked closely at the letters she was given to file. It seems that your Dr McGordon, under the name of Donald Mortimer, is very interested in Casa Machico. He has already spoken to the authorities about his intention of using it as a nursing home for cancer patients and there are no objections. There is, however, one problem. The property is for sale but the two doctors wish to rent or – what is your word? – or lease it.'

'Of course they would,' Luke exclaimed. 'Now that you mention it, it's obvious. Once they stepped outside the law, they would not want a large sum of money tied up where they could not recover it without being traced. On the other hand, if they are to conduct surgical operations they will need to carry out improvements. They would prefer that the building owner pays for the improvements but I don't suppose that he will see it quite that way. Do we know who owns the property?'

Carlos glanced down at a small notebook. 'The property belongs to an Englishman, a Senhor Edward Gentle who lives in Crawley. He lived there for many years, with his brother and both their families, but now it is too big for what remains of the families and he has returned to where he was born, this place with the unpleasant name. He wishes to sell.'

Luke sat up straight. An idea was beginning to germinate. 'Carlos,' he said, 'how does this Mr Gentle communicate with his *advogado*?'

'I will find out.'

'If it's by email – you know about emails?' (Carlos sneered as if to say that every intelligent person knew about emails.) 'Good. I'll need to know the email address of the lawyers and of Mr Gentle. Your fiancée will be willing to find this out?'

Carlos smiled complacently.

'Good,' Luke said. 'She will then have fulfilled her part of the bargain.'

He escaped as soon as good manners and Portuguese formality would allow and hurried back to his hotel room where he began the composition and encryption of a long and complex email to Honeypot.

By the afternoon of the following day Luke was in a position to email to Honeypot:

Casa Machico belongs to an Englishman, Mr Gentle, who lives in Crawley. He is anxious to sell and for the moment will not hear of rental. I understand that once in the past he suffered with a bad tenant. Your quarry, for reasons that you will understand, is unwilling to commit capital to a purchase.

See the attachment for full names and email or other addresses of those concerned.

You will have noted that Crawley is no great distance from Gatwick Airport.

How you proceed is up to you but I would suggest an email ostensibly from Mr Gentle to the lawyer, agreeing to discuss renting Casa Machico, but only face to face with the prospective tenant. He would be willing to come to Gatwick Airport and meet the trio for a serious discussion. He wishes to see what sort of people he would be trusting with his building and possibly his reputation. He also want details of what alterations they would make and a deposit against dilapidations. Your doctors will not miss the point that they need not leave the airport at all but could return to Madeira the same evening or next morning at the latest.

That may fetch them back. It's the most I can do, take it or leave it. I'm catching the next convenient plane home and will advise you when to send a car for us.

A terse note from Honeypot acknowledged the information and advice without further comment.

Two more days passed. A football match, of great importance to those who were interested in such events, was taking place in Lisbon. Aircraft were diverted to ferry the extra traffic and were replaced on their scheduled routes by smaller planes. A backlog of passengers to other destinations accumulated. Luke could have rested and basked in the shade around the pools but his mind was too caught up with other matters. Then the match took place. Portugal lost. The airlines were now much less interested in furthering the interests of the football enthusiasts. They were, after all, assured of their patronage at some date because even football supporters have to go home eventually. Seats became available.

Jane's farewell to each of her new friends

took the form of a speech in fluent Portuguese, carefully composed and translated with the aid of her dictionary and one of the busboys and then learned by heart. Luke and Jane were again booked into first class and travelled in less than the usual squalor. Jane, still ruffled after a tussle with Security, who had confiscated a very small and half-empty bottle of shampoo, claimed the window seat. She looked down at the Ponto do Rosto as it fell behind them and sighed. 'That's the end of a perfect holiday,' she said.

'I'm glad that you've enjoyed it,' said her great-grandfather. 'So now it's back to rainy old Britain.' He composed himself for a nap. He had been unsettled by a glimpse of the two doctors at Funchal Airport but he had seen no sign of them boarding the same plane. Presumably they were going directly to Gatwick. Or maybe they had taken fright and were heading for pastures new.

'The fine weather's come back,' Jane said. 'Aunt Helena's last email said so. Or do I start calling her Mum?'

Luke yawned. 'Whatever she says.' He composed himself to doze but was unable to snatch more than occasional moments of repose. Things would be happening when they landed but he would not be able to witness any of them. Even a verbatim report by Honeypot, if she so favoured him, would not be quite the same. He had been looking forward to a restful period but now he wanted to be part of the action.

Luke had been worrying about journeying home from Glasgow Airport. Had Honeypot used her much vaunted clout to get them returned to Newton Lauder by Traffic car? As the plane came out of cloud and circled the toylike airport before landing he saw the livery of a police car, tucked tightly against the wall of the nearest terminal building, so he could relax at last.

He relaxed too soon. When the doors were opened, they were whisked off the plane by a police presence of two uniformed officers. There was a distinct drawing-aside by other passengers. Bypassing all formalities beyond a glance at their passports and a cursory baggage check they were chivvied into another and smaller plane, tourist class this time. Doors were slammed behind them. They found their seats. Honeypot and another officer were seated across the aisle with a bandaged figure between them.

'Roddy?' Jane asked uncertainly.

'Jane!' Roddy's identification was more positive.

'Roddy!' Jane pushed past Luke, stretched over Honeypot and grasped Roddy's hands. Between the two, Honeypot was becoming disarranged – a state to which she was not accustomed. To the dismay of the cabin crew, who were trying to get all passengers seated and strapped in for takeoff, Jane insisted on sitting beside Roddy, which necessitated Honeypot moving across the aisle. Luke moved to the window seat. As the last seat belt clicked home, the plane began its takeoff run.

Roddy and Jane had not released each other's hands but Luke decided not to cavil about it. 'What the hell's going on?' he asked Honeypot.

Detective Chief Inspector Laird looked at him in surprise. 'My last email must have missed you,' she said. 'But you could have worked it out for yourself. After all, you almost masterminded it. The two men and possibly the woman as well are on a plane that will arrive at Gatwick before we touch down or possibly shortly afterwards, depending on the wind and whether there's any waiting around for people making connections.'

'We're on the shuttle? Nobody tells me anything.'

'Welcome to the club,' said Honeypot. 'Yes, this is the shuttle.' They had crossed the Border and were over England before she said, 'You've settled one question for me. I was puzzled by your Mr Blantyre's statement that there was another hospice or nursing home abroad. I wondered why they didn't just go there to hide out. Their anxiety to acquire another such premises in Madeira settled it. There never was such a place. Enquiries confirm that several well-heeled and apparently healthy patients were confirmed as having cancer and were shipped abroad in the care of the nurse – to North Africa, we believe. Nothing was ever heard of them again. The Algerian police have a source that suggests that they were quietly put to sleep by lethal injection and buried at a site near El Asnam. Exhumations are being arranged although whether after this time in a hot climate it would still be possible to detect whether any of them did in fact have cancer is open to doubt. Given new nursing facilities in Madeira, they need not be bothered if we were to close down the Yardstone House operation. They could find their patients online and let them come direct to them abroad.'

Luke made no comment. He was too appalled in considering the implications of what he had just been told.

At Gatwick, they were bundled into a waiting, liveried police car for the change of terminals. There Luke, Jane and Honeypot were escorted into a bright room overlooking a runway. The room was triple-glazed against the aircraft noise so that planes ghosted by like gliders. The two doctors, known to Honeypot as Dr McGordon and Mr Samson but to Luke as Charles Hopgood and Mr Buckley, were already seated by the window under the eye of two local police in plain clothes – a tough-looking sergeant and, for the look of it, a woman detective chief inspector. The two female officers greeted each other warmly and Luke recalled hearing that Honeypot had begun her career with the Met.

Honeypot nodded Luke and Jane to seats and took up a stand in front of the two accused men. 'Well, well!' she said. 'Dr McGordon AKA Charles Hopgood and AKA Donald Mortimer, accompanied by Mr Samson, AKA Mr Buckley.'

The larger of the men said 'We deny being any of those people. This is a clear case of mistaken identity.' The two men seemed to radiate venom. Jane took hold of Luke's hand.

The local DCI said 'Perhaps you'd like to see the passports they were travelling with? According to those, they are George Ross and William Jenkins.'

'There you are, then,' said the larger man.

The DCI, in a bored voice, said, 'The photographs had been substituted. We are checking on when and where the passports were stolen and I should hear back from the passport office in a few minutes.'

Honeypot took the two passports, placed a handkerchief that looked like silk over each photograph in turn and then ran a thumb over it. 'Genuine but stolen,' she confirmed. 'You can feel the line where the plastic was once slit. You agree?'

'That was my own conclusion.'

'That's good enough to hold them on. I identify this man as being Dr Duncan McGordon, formerly of Edinburgh,' said Honeypot, 'and the other as Mr Samson, surgeon, also formerly of Edinburgh.' She looked round. 'Where is the woman?'

The local DCI was frowning into a large envelope. 'Nobody said anything to me about a woman, just the two men. But there

251

seems to be a third passport here.'

Honeypot took the extra passport and studied the photograph. 'This is not Mrs Dulcie McGordon.'

'My wife,' said Dr McGordon, 'left me more than two years ago and went to her sister in Canada, as you were well aware. I have not seen her since.'

'Then you admit to being Dr McGordon?' There was no answer. 'Never mind. DNA, fingerprints and biometrics will settle the matter.' Honeypot's lip curled. 'If we dig up one of your gardens, will we find your wife?'

The doctor grinned triumphantly. 'Go ahead,' he said. 'I never owned a garden. If you're referring to the lady who accompanied us on Madeira, she was just a friend. We left her on the island. And if you've been messing around with her passport it looks as though she'll have to stay there.'

Honeypot knew that she'd made a mistake. 'When you lived next door to me—'

'That house was rented.'

Honeypot abandoned what was going to become an unprofitable line of questioning. 'Please explain how her passport comes to be here,' she said, 'if the lady never left Madeira.' There was no answer. She nodded to her companion who had been making notes in a competent-looking shorthand. He laid aside his pocketbook and went to the door. He returned and escorted the figure of Roddy to a seat. The two medical men looked unsurprised; Roddy's rescue and survival had been well publicized.

Honeypot asked, 'Do you recognize these two men?'

Roddy's bandages nodded. 'Mr Hopgood and Mr Buckley.'

'No comment,' the two men said in unison. 'Not until our solicitor is present,' Dr McGordon added.

'Mr McWilliam, please tell us in your own words what happened at Wellborn Farm. Never mind for the moment what led up to those events.'

The boy nodded again. His voice was husky but calm and dispassionate. 'I believed that they were pursuing me. I could hear somebody behind me as I reached Wellborn. I went to run across the courtyard, intending to double round the far side and hide myself in what was left of the byre. The ground gave way under my feet. It was an old well, covered by heavy boards that had rotted, though I didn't know that at the time. I went down the well, feet first, until I stuck. I had given my head several hard knocks and my chest was being squeezed but I didn't black out for a minute or so. Looking upward, I could recognize the heads of these two men. And I couldn't make out what they said but I knew their voices because of their connection with Kempfield.' Roddy's voice hardened. 'Then a torch shone on me and a third voice spoke. It said. "Just leave him there. They won't find him and he'll be dead within a day or so. That won't count as murder." '

'And whose voice was it?' Honeypot asked.

'It was the woman I knew as Mrs Hopgood. Then Mr Hopgood said that perhaps they should drop a large stone on top of me to make sure and the woman's voice asked how that would be compatible with an accident. Then I blacked out. I had a few conscious moments after that but I couldn't tell which were real and which were hallucinations.'

There was a momentary flurry of movement. Dr McGordon was a large man and had always exuded an impression of ruthless power. Now he seemed to have lost power and, with it, bulk. That may be why it had not been seen necessary to handcuff him. He struggled to his feet against restraining hands. He seemed to be on the point of uttering threats and the policeman with the pocket-book readied his pencil. But the doctor deflated again.

'You will swear to that on oath?'

'I certainly will,' Roddy said.

There were a few seconds of hostility that seemed to roll around the room like a heavy gas. Then Honeypot began to recite the statutory warning.

FOURTEEN

The two prisoners were spirited away, to be returned to Scotland by unspecified means. Honeypot also vanished with her old friend, taking Roddy with them. It was understood that statements were being taken but Luke and Jane, once they had made positive identifications, were not for the moment required. They were left to make their own way home, without any offer to ease their travel or to fund their fares. It is generally assumed that to have helped the police in the general direction of justice is recompense enough. Any swing of the pendulum towards treating the public with consideration has been slow and its effect localized. They flew back tourist, amid noisy babies, overweight ladies and men who had been kept waiting rather too long in the bar.

No obliging police cars appeared to transport them but Luke, forewarned of this, had made good use of his mobile phone from Gatwick and Helena arrived in the Terios before they had cleared the carousel. Luke pleaded exhaustion and a total amnesia on the subject of driving so that Helena had to take the wheel again. While she drove she was treated to a terse and garbled summary of the adventures of the two wanderers during their absence. They got home late, hungry and exhausted but at least they were home. Circe greeted Luke with affection but she was distraught with pleasure at Jane's safe return and Jane was delighted that Circe's training had been kept up and her weight down. Violet's pleasure was less noticeable; from having the full attention of Roddy she now had to share him with a sister to whom Roddy acknowledged a major debt. Sisterly affection could be seen to be at a low ebb.

Angela's ankle would not yet bear her weight and the doctors were not going to release her into society until it could be expected to withstand careful use. Roddy was therefore still in the care of Helena, who was in a tizzy of anxiety about him; but Luke insisted that the Met could be trusted to see that he was returned to them in one piece.

When he made that statement Luke had his fingers crossed but it proved to be correct. Luke and Jane had slept the sleep of exhaustion. When Roddy was returned by police car they were giving Helena and Violet a more reasoned and less accurate account of their travels while making up for a day survived on little but airline food. Roddy, when delivered to their doorstep, had already had a good breakfast but, being young and male, he was quite ready for another one. They all settled down together in the kitchen, amid the debris of previous breakfasts, while Roddy ate. His memory was now fully restored and, between mouthfuls, he told the full story of the fateful day much as he had told it in his formal statement to Honeypot.

Roddy, as surmised, had called at Kempfield to satisfy himself that his work of earlier in the day was up to his standard and the glue setting satisfactorily. He took a good look and all was well. On his way out he decided to call at the office to hand in as lost property a penknife that somebody had left behind on a workbench. He had chosen his moment badly. The two doctors had evidently thought that they had that part of the building to themselves. Roddy, with quite unnecessary conformity, went to sign himself both in and out in the attendance book, which lived during the day on a shelf in the hallway but was kept overnight in the office. In crêpe-soles shoes and moving on terrazzo tiles (the latter having been surplus from the construction of a shopping centre complex) he made no sound. The office door was open and voices were raised in argument. As the treasurer reached the doorway he was looking into Roddy's face while at the same moment the director, behind him, was crying out that 'It's too late for that. People have died and we'll be held responsible.'

Even then, the words had no significance for Roddy. If the director had just nodded and walked past, he would have thought no more about it, at least until the background began to emerge. But Dr McGordon (or Mr

Hopgood, as Roddy knew him) threw the words 'Shut up, you idiot' over his shoulder, hesitated for a second and then jumped towards the boy. Roddy had no idea what was going on but he could recognize a threatening movement when he saw it directed at him. He never could say how he knew that the threat was serious, but luckily he leaped to the right conclusion and fled. The treasurer was between him and the main door, so he darted through the woodwork shop and threw himself against the panic bolts and out onto the grass beyond.

After covering a hundred yards at full tilt he slowed and looked back, but saw nothing to encourage him to stop and parley. The treasurer was emerging from the same fire escape door, his expression and attitude still showing menace. Roddy could see past the side of the building and the manager was out in the car park. His attitude was no more reassuring. Abandoning his mother's car to any interested joyrider, Roddy slipped through a hedge and hurdled a fence. After crossing the first field he seemed to have shaken off pursuit. They could still intercept him on the way to his mother's house so he headed instead for Luke's. What he forgot, however, was that the farm road, after it had passed Luke's house, had most of his route in view although the viewers' car would be largely hidden by hedges. It emerged later that his two pursuers, chauffeured by the woman who had been waiting in their car, had taken that road and had got ahead of him. Just as he was entering the courtyard of Wellborn Farm the men jumped out at him from what remained of the old barn. But a startled youth has better acceleration than one or even two middle-aged men of sedentary habit. Roddy shot across the courtyard, well clear of any pursuit, but the violence of his panicking footsteps was too much for the rotten boards. People, Roddy pointed out, were often said to have wished for the ground to open and swallow them up but he was virtually unique in having experienced it. As his strength was returning so also was his sense of humour. Both girls laughed obligingly.

His recollection of the fall was complete and he told the story in great detail. He was aware of falling and of hitting his head several times on the way down the well. Even as he fell he was also aware of the danger of water below, but at least he was spared that; scarcity of water had been a major reason why the farm had been given up. He retained consciousness for long enough to hear the woman's damning remark. This was followed by a blank of many days.

That tale told, Roddy reached for the cereal packets. He seemed to be preparing for a third breakfast, leaving Luke and Helena to argue over where he was to sleep now that Jane and Luke were home. It was soon agreed that Jane and Violet would have to share a bedroom, a decision that brought in its train the advantage that neither was going to allow the other to stray in the night. At the same time, Luke was relieved for the moment of the burden of having to play the heavy great-grandfather.

Later that day, Honeypot paid a call and found Luke alone. She had the grace to offer a word of thanks for his assistance and of apology for deserting him in London, but only half a word on each subject. Apology sticks in the throat of most police officers.

'We've identified the woman at last,' she said. 'Her name is Agnes Fulsom. She was a nursing sister at the clinic where they carried out their unhallowed surgery. In fact, it seems that she diverted into their clutches several patients with organ failure or who believed themselves to have malignant growths. There could be no doubt that she was as guilty as either of the men and she fled when they did. Elementary arithmetic applied to certain balance transfers suggests that she was collecting a one-third share. She's still on the loose but we'll catch up with her, have no fear. There's no call for you to worry about her.'

'Why should I worry?' Luke asked. He had rarely worried about a woman. None of them had ever meant him any harm – the reverse, in fact.

Honeypot shrugged. 'From what we've been able to learn, she's a really bad one. In addition to the trafficking in human organs, certain documents have been turning up – wills and insurance policies in favour of any one of the three culprits in particular. There is now a very strong suspicion that after any such formalities had been completed, she was not above giving the patient a helping hand into eternity. It seems to have been sex that drove her on,' Honeypot said austerely, 'in her relentless pursuit of money. Unless you happen to be beautiful or famous, preferably both, a hyperactive sex life requires some financial clout. But she's dropped out of sight. We think she's abroad again...'

Nearly a week later, Angela was out of hospital and managing very well. Roddy had therefore gone home although with some reluctance. He had enjoyed having two attractive girls mooning and squabbling over him and was not looking forward to nursemaiding his mother, but he was left in no doubt that the bed that he had occupied was needed for Violet and that he was not going to remain to share it.

That afternoon, Luke decided to take a seat outside. He had put in several hours, waterproofing the roofs of his shed and garage against the foreseeable winter, using bitumen. He was tired. Not just physically tired from his efforts with the tar-brush but tired through and through. He thought that he had been around for too long. Waking up at all was a huge effort, to be rewarded by another day of sleepiness, stiffness and labour. Perhaps tomorrow he wouldn't bother. There would be a lot to be said for perpetual sleep.

A brisk breeze had sprung up but round the corner from the terrace was a sheltered corner. He settled down there and began to ponder. His train of thought was unusually glum. Who, if anyone, would be the worse if he refused to awake next morning? Helena would miss her marriage but he had already made provision for her in his will. She would go without her sex, but he was finding even his best simulation of sex to be too much of a chore and he had a suspicion that she was only pretending pleasure for his sake. Jane would genuinely miss him, but she was becoming more fiercely independent every day. Helena could cope with her. It seemed that Violet would soon have Roddy to look after her.

He sank deeper into gloom. From where he sat he could see where his own dog, Pepper, now lay buried in her favourite place beneath the maple. She had been his dog-of-a-lifetime and he still felt privileged to have had her. He had never managed to use a shotgun with any degree of skill but the lack of one eye was little handicap when it came to the use of a small-bore rifle and he also enjoyed picking-up on local shoots. They had developed that intuitive mutual understanding that develops, in special cases, between dog and handler. While they waited for action she could tuck herself so totally out of sight that sometimes he was tempted to believe that she had wandered off. She knew what he would want before he knew it himself and often he knew that she had sensed the approach of a quarry before he was aware of her reaction. Whenever he was out of her sight, she pined. Was she now dreaming, he wondered, in her long sleep? Dreaming perhaps of days spent stalking the hedgerows alone together and perfectly happy. Would she be waiting to jump up at him – the one bad habit that he had never managed to break? If he could be sure of that, he would not hesitate to go now.

Sensing his unhappiness, Circe appeared and laid her head on his knee. He pulled her ears and massaged her scalp. She was a loving and lovely dog but she was not Pepper.

So what did life still have to offer him? Increasing stiffness until he was confined to his armchair, dependent on his womenfolk to put on his socks and to tie his shoelaces for him. Loss of faculties. He had already had far more than his threescore and ten. His contemporary friends had all gone before or vanished into care homes. Younger men had their own friends and talked shop in languages that he did not know. Old age was a lonely place.

His deliberations had reached that point when he heard voices from the bedroom window above his head, the room that the girls had been sharing. 'Just you keep away from him, that's all,' said Violet.

Jane's voice sounded superior and amused. 'I haven't seen your name branded on his backside.'

There was a pause while Violet assumed an equally supercilious voice. 'When, may I ask, did you ever set eyes on Roddy's bum?' she asked.

Jane had no need of words. She produced a laugh so dirty that it almost carried conviction, even to her great-grandfather.

Violet wasted some seconds in search of a suitably devastating and sophisticated response. 'You'll be sorry,' she said at last, her voice rising. 'I've had enough of you hanging around Roddy, wiggling and pouting and reminding him that you went down the well. You're making a fool of yourself and people are talking. You're too young to be playing that sort of game.'

'But it seems that I'm better at it than you are. Roddy seems to think so. Hadn't we better leave it to him to make up his own mind?'

'No. He might get it wrong.' For a moment the hardness left Violet's voice and there was a trace of amusement.

'I think you're afraid that he might get it right.'

Any amusement in Violet's voice vanished. 'That's just about the wrong side of enough. You keep clear or else.'

Jane could be heard to yawn. 'I'm shaking in my shoes,' she said. 'Or else what?'

'Or else you won't like it. I'll tell Roddy what you said about him.'

'I didn't say anything about him.'

'I know that,' said Violet. 'You know it. But Roddy doesn't know it. I can tell him whatever I like. He'll hate you.'

'If we're playing that sort of game,' Jane said slowly, 'that's probably another game that I'm better at than you are. Come to think of it, yes. You'll be amazed when you hear what you said about Roddy. He'll put you down as a foul-mouthed scrubber—'

'Oh yes? I wonder which of us he'll believe.'

'He may believe the one who went down the well for him.'

'You little bitch! You're going to grow into a slut. I'm going to tell GG that he'll have to change his will. I'm not going to accept responsibility for you, not ever. He'll have to think of something else.' Voices were rising. Luke judged that the moment when slapping and hair-pulling, if not worse, would begin was not far off. He heard cloth rip. Luke raised his own voice. 'Break it up, you two! I'm not going yet.'

An appalled silence was broken at last by Jane's voice. 'There now!' she said. 'See what you've done!'

Violet's voice went up to what in anyone less attractive would have been called a screech. 'What *I've* done? Who started it by ... by slobbering and drooling over the boy who...? I—'

'That is enough and more than enough,' Luke said. 'Not another word out of either of you. Come down here, and quietly, right now.'

If challenged, he would have had to admit to being astonished when both girls arrived in front of him only seconds later. Their demeanour was such that they might have been arriving before the desk of a head-mistress. Each looked dishevelled. Violet's old summer frock showed a long rip with white cotton peeping through. There were tears on Jane's face. Neither wished to be the first to speak.

Luke said, 'I neither know nor care who started this particular argument. What I do know is that I am not going to spend my declining years, perhaps my declining days or even, for all I know, my declining minutes being disturbed by futile squabbling over a matter that is of little interest to anyone but your two selves except in giving rise to amusement. No amount of argument between the two of you is likely to have the slightest effect on Roddy's ultimate choice, except to scunner him of the pair of you. Roddy is the only person who could say which of you he prefers and I doubt very much that he'd be fool enough to tell you.'

Jane found her voice. 'We could go and ask him,' she said. Violet nodded. The two girls began to turn.

'Stop!' Luke's voice froze them in mid-pirouette. 'One, Roddy and his mother are in Peebles today. Two, you're going to mow the grass, both of you, working as a team, turnabout, one mowing and one emptying the hopper and turning over the compost. And I don't want to hear a single word more on the subject –' Luke hid a smile '– until Roddy comes to me to ask for the hand of one of you in marriage. And at that time I shall ask him whether he's really thought what he's doing. Now go.'

The two turned away, arguing in whispers, but they headed for the old summerhouse where the mower was waiting.

Luke's contemplative mood was gone. The breeze was colder and it had backed so that it was finding its way into his nook. He picked up his chair, returned it to the terrace and entered the house through the French windows. He was coming out of bright sunshine and the curtains were partly closed. He had crossed the shaded kitchen and was seating himself in the old basket chair that had been a favourite of his mother's and of his wife and was now his favourite too. He was lowering himself into its seat with a creaking that had been a welcome part of his childhood when a woman's voice spoke from the shadows. 'Good!' she said. 'I was just wondering how to bring you inside. I want a word with you.' As his eyes adjusted to the dimness he saw that she was holding a shotgun under her armpit. She looked as though she knew how to use it.

FIFTEEN

Luke had only seen the woman in the distance, usually when she brought their car to collect her collaborators from Kempfield or once in the street and flanked by the two men. Seen close to and alone, once his heart rate had steadied, he sensed rather than saw, being unable to get an all-round view, that she was sturdily built and slightly stout with a prominent bosom but small buttocks. Her jacket and skirt fitted her slightly top-heavy figure too well to have been bought off the peg. There might just possibly have been time to have them made since her return to Britain. However, while Luke was no fashion expert, Helena and the two girls insisted on catching any fashion programme on the sitting room television and Luke was usually too tired or lazy to disturb himself in order to watch something else on the kitchen set. The cut of her jacket and skirt struck him as being slightly dated, although he could not

271

have said how. This suggested a secret repository somewhere in Britain from which she had been able to recover clothes, money and possibly the shotgun. Her hair was light brown, almost blonde, very thick and long enough to drape over her shoulders. He put her age at thirty-five.

The shotgun was of high quality. The loss of his right eye during his army days more than sixty years earlier had put the efficient use of a shotgun beyond Luke's capability and he was too much of a perfectionist to accept doing something badly. All the same, he was familiar enough with the subject to realize that it was not a lady's gun, if for no other reason than that it had been built for somebody with longer arms. He thought that it might be the property of one of the men, left in the same store in order to bypass any difficulty over taking firearms abroad. He was sure that he recalled the financial director – Dr McGordon as he now knew him to be – shooting very competently at driven pheasants on one of the shoots where Luke was picking up. The polished walnut stock gleamed softly. The blueing was unmarked.

His photographer's eye left him in little doubt that her attractive and slightly fragile expression was the result of highly skilled make-up. Beneath it he could detect a face that was cold and strong-featured, with lips that were not quite as full as they were painted. The eyes which, similarly, were narrower than they first appeared, were regarding him as they might an insect in a killing bottle. Luke suppressed a small shiver that tried to run up his back.

'I've been waiting for you to come inside,' she said.

Her accent was neutral. Her voice was slightly husky but without any hint of sexuality. It was the huskiness of acute nervous tension and he did not like it. 'Why was that?' he asked, for something to say.

'To get you alone, one at a time. You know who I am?'

'I can guess. You're not very like your picture.'

'The picture that you helped them to concoct after I'd been careful to keep my face away from your camera.' Luke shook his head but she ignored it. 'Between the lot of you, you've sunk me good and proper. And my friends. I had my life organized just the way I wanted it but now ... You owe me a life.'

Luke's mouth had dried but he took a few

seconds to find some saliva. He decided that as long as he could keep her talking he could postpone whatever else was to follow. Also he would have admitted to a soupçon of curiosity. 'You say your friends. Or do you mean lovers?'

She shrugged. 'Call them whatever you like. I don't suppose they'll give a fish's fart.'

'In your book there's no difference? Does that mean that becoming your friend means becoming your lover? Or that your lovers end up as your friends?' She only looked unconcerned so he felt compelled to press on. 'Your lovers, then. Both of them? At the same time?'

She nodded to each of his questions with a smirk of barely concealed pride. It struck him as resembling the *somebody-loves-me* pride that a mother with a new baby can never quite hide. But her eyes were looking at him as though he were mad. Perhaps, he thought, mad was just what he was. He had a light-headed sense of unreality, which may have been saving his sanity by cushioning it. 'Not that it's any of your damn business,' she said.

'But you're good?'

'You'll never know.' She scowled at him, an expression that seemed to sit more naturally on her features than the smirk. 'What business of yours was it that we were making money off people who'd been let down by the NHS? And who were going to die anyway. They were as good as dead.'

Her colossal gall in blaming the National Health Service for crimes on her part that came very close to or even included murder, took his breath away. He leaned back, crossed his knees and laced his hands together – anything to encourage a conversational attitude. And then he could not think of anything to say except on the one subject that would have been better avoided. 'You and your lovers,' he said, 'tried to kill a boy who had become very dear to my whole family – who, indeed, looks very much like becoming part of my family. After one of my girls rescued him, it was inevitable that we would learn the whole story. When the police inspector asked for my help, I could hardly refuse.'

Her scowl looked darker. 'And she's another one,' she said. 'The female fuzz. Another one that I'll have to kill. I can use one of those girls as bait to bring her here.'

The shiver up his back was in danger of becoming a tremor. He could be sure that she had passed over some barrier and was in a world of her own, lost to reason and conscience. Talk of killing in some other backyard would have had less impact, but here in his own secluded retreat where the world never made an appearance ... But he had to go on or he was sure that he would die. The sound of the mower had stopped. What were they doing now? 'Why do you have to go about killing people?' he asked gently. 'Have you killed already?'

She shook her head. 'It doesn't matter. Why should I be different from my friends?'

'Killing can't do you any good. It won't get you out of trouble. Too much is known already and you can't kill everybody in the world. They'll get you—'

'They'll get me anyway,' she said. He saw her forefinger tighten on the trigger and his stomach prepared to leap aside even if he couldn't follow. She seated herself on the corner of the kitchen table, which gave him half a fighting chance. Her skirt rode up to show a wrinkle in the fine nylon above her knee. Unobtrusively, he uncrossed his knees. There was a loud report from the garden and he nearly bit his tongue. So Jane was giving Circe a retrieve or two with the dummy launcher. When his heartbeat had slowed for the second time, he leaned forward in an attitude that could have been taken as a gesture of intimacy.

'Their trials are bound to bring out all the details,' she said, 'and it's the sort of story that gets the public steamed up just because they think that it's the sort of thing that they wouldn't do. They're jealous, of course. Nonentities are always jealous of somebodies. Jealous of anyone who has the guts to step out of the ruck and grab what's there for the grabbing.'

'You could still run,' Luke said. 'But not if you stir up too much of a hornet's nest, of course. Or don't you have a spare passport?'

'I could get another passport,' she said. 'But I don't have half enough money to go on the run.'

'You must have made more than enough over the years. What have you spent it on?' His question was in part conversational but he was also curious.

'Nothing that you and your respectable, hidebound, boring friends would approve of.' She paused and for a moment a faint smile touched her thin lips. It was not a nice smile. 'But by God I've enjoyed it. Maybe it's all been worthwhile. I've had money. Never let them tell you that money doesn't bring happiness. If you've got money you'll have friends and if you've got friends you can find contentment. But now I've nowhere to go and I'm buggered if I'm going to spend my best years behind bars or scraping by in some rotten hole. I'd rather kill myself but I'll take with me the ones who brought us all down. Then I'll have something to chuckle over with my friends when we meet up again on the other side.'

He was trying to memorize her words but her gestures were becoming less controlled and he was becoming ever more scared. 'Would you please take your finger off that trigger,' he said hoarsely. 'One sneeze and you could blow me in half.'

'Now or later,' she said, 'who cares?'

Luke decided that he cared very much. A few minutes earlier, in the grip of depression, he had almost decided that ageing pains and the foreshortening of the view ahead made living barely worth the struggle. He had reconciled himself, at the best, to a lingering old age in an armchair, living vicariously. But now he wanted to see another spring, to marry Helena and to lead at least one of his great-granddaughters down the aisle. He wanted to look up old friends – there must be one or two still alive somewhere – and do a pub-crawl even if it had to be in a bath chair. He wanted to tell his doctor to find some way to lubricate his joints. His much-loved Pepper could wait a little longer to be reunited.

'You don't want to kill me,' he said hoarsely.

She leered at him. 'I do. Very much. Give me one reason why I shouldn't.'

For one moment he thought that his mind had died on him and that the rest of him was as good as dead. Then an idea staggered back into his mind. He had discarded it earlier because surely she would never believe it. Unless she wanted to believe it, of course. It might not work but it was all there was. 'You think you're good,' he said. 'The greatest courtesan since Aphrodite. But I'm *bloody* good.' It was a forlorn hope but it seemed to be worth a try.

'You're an old man,' she said contemptuously.

'Old means experienced. Did you never hear the saying about the best tunes being played on an old fiddle? When you lived here, did you not hear the gossip?'

Luke's wife had died young. He had continued living in what had always been his family's home. This was secluded from the view of neighbours, so that a lady might approach it, confident that she was un-observed. His rugged looks had worn well and had been embellished rather than blemished by the eyepatch that he wore in the very cold or very dry weather in which his empty eye socket tended to become dry and raw. The houses in the nearest offshoot from the town were small and tended to attract widows and divorcees. Until the un-expected arrival into his care of his great-granddaughters, Luke had never been short of female companionship of the other sort, although the gossip about him had far exceeded reality.

There had been no more reports from the dummy launcher. He felt that he was being observed through the screen of cotoneaster that sheltered the terrace. But perhaps that was wishful thinking. He had caught the woman's interest. 'Luke Grant? You're *that* Luke Grant?'

He nodded. He decided he would throw himself on the gun rather than allow any harm to come to either of the girls. He summoned up the memory of lust so that he could pretend it. He narrowed his eyes, slightly flared his nostrils and moistened his lips. 'When they were handing out geriatric impotence,' he said, 'they never came to me.

I don't know why. Just lucky I suppose. Or perhaps I was hiding behind the door, as they say. How about it?' he asked. 'I can still promise a lady an orgasm that'll come out of her ears in the form of smoke-filled bubbles. My God, what a couple we'd make!'

Her face became a hardened mask. 'You think I'm daft? It's impossible. I'm not giving you a chance to grab this gun.'

He needed a little longer. There was a shadow moving on the terrace. What images might appeal to her? 'If you tied my hands behind me...'

The thought was new and exciting. Her breathing quickened, her eyes had a new sparkle and she began to move rhythmically on the corner of the table. She was calling up a mental picture. He turned his mind away quickly from what fantasies might be fermenting in her sick mind. There was a drop of saliva at the corner of her mouth. She looked round the kitchen. 'What with?'

He was still stumbling along, solving each problem as she threw it at him. 'Your tights will have to come off anyway.'

She let the gun's muzzle drop as she considered. An eye was peeping round the corner of the wall beside the French windows. It seemed that his proposition might be accepted. He just hoped that something would interrupt before he had to live up to his boast. It had been fifteen years since erectile dysfunction had struck. He would just have to continue the bluff until the last possible second and pray that he would be given a chance to grab for the gun, or else that someone or something would intervene.

The woman stood. Behind her, she was managing to work her tights down one-handed. There might never come a better moment. She must have followed his glance at the door. Whether or not she had sensed danger, she began to turn and raise the gun.

He must, he simply must, command her attention at whatever cost. 'Now,' he shouted. 'Now.' At the same moment he hurled himself forward. He had not believed that his elderly muscles and stiff joints could manage such a leap.

The creak of the basket chair was like the cry of a lost soul. He seemed to be travelling very slowly and yet he was flying, defying gravity like a glider. The gun was wrenched back towards him. He slapped at the muzzles, careful to keep his fingers out of harm's way though what good they would be to him in his grave he would not have cared to guess.

The noise of the gun in the confined space was stunning on its own. But he was aware of a massive hammer-blow to his side that span him round and deposited him on the floor, winded and in agony. For the moment, he was a spectator.

The sound of the shotgun was followed instantly by another higher, lighter sound. The woman staggered and span round. The shotgun fell beside him with a clatter, pointing into his face. Something else bounced off a high cupboard, span and clattered into the sink. Jane had zapped the woman with a dummy from the launcher. The two-pound dummy could deliver a heavy blow but not enough to stun. Luke was only too well aware that only one barrel of the shotgun had been fired and, as part of his mind came back from its confusion, he had time to bless the quality of the gun and the maker who would have fitted intercepting sears, preventing the other barrel being fired by the jolt when it was dropped. He tried to roll on to the gun but the movement hurt too much.

The two girls arrived and hit the woman like a pair of Rugby players. Just for once they made a formidable team, co-ordinated and synchronized. They were dragging the woman backwards. She tried to resist but her tights were tripping her and she lost her footing and fell back. The last he saw from his unusual angle was a pair of feet sliding towards the door, leaving behind a smart pair of court shoes. There were voices but his ears were still deafened from the double blast. The room reeked of cordite.

'Don't kill her,' he shouted. To himself his voice was muffled. Calling out sent pulses of agony through his chest. He only hoped that neither of them would be daft enough to let the woman go in order to tend to his injuries.

Very tentatively he moved a hand to where he had been hit. He would not have been surprised to find half his ribs missing – at such close quarters a twelve-bore shotgun firing more than an ounce of shot can do terrible damage. There was certainly a wound. He jerked his fingers away from a gap that felt spongy with at least one sharp splinter protruding. It was serious but not as serious as it might have been and he guessed that he had almost got out of the way of most of the shot charge. But he was sure that two or three ribs were damaged and one was broken. Whether any ricochets had gone inward, time would tell. There was a lot of blood but none of it seemed to be getting into his lungs. A clean dishtowel was within reach. He pulled it down with his good hand and packed it into and around the wound. He pulled the leg of a chair closer with the opposite hand, to hold it in place.

His mobile phone had come out of his pocket. He managed to key nine-nine-nine. The pain was becoming unendurable but when a voice answered he was surprised to find how calm and clear his voice had become.

A little later the two girls returned. They looked terrified. 'I've phoned for an ambulance,' he whispered. 'There's nothing more for you to do. Just look after each other and explain to Helena when she gets back. What did you do with that hellcat?'

'We tied her to a tree,' Jane said simply. There were tears on her face and her voice was shaking but she was holding herself together. 'Are you all right, GG? No, I know you're not all right but will you be?'

Nature's anaesthesia was taking over as shock worked its magic on his body chemistry. The pain was less but speech still hurt his chest. He forced his mind to work.

'Called the ambulance,' he repeated. 'Be

here in five minutes. Only got to come down the hill. Make sure front door's open then get back to her. Nothing else for you to do here. Mustn't get away. Could kill some-body else.'

'She won't,' Violet said. 'Even if she unties herself the police can find her in minutes. We tarred and feathered her.'

This seemed perfectly logical but there were certain gaps in the story. 'On top of her clothes?'

'Of course not, GG,' said Jane. 'That would have been silly and it would have made it easy for her to get it off. We used the last of your bitumen and – I'm sorry – we ripped up a cushion from the sitting room. Was that all right?'

Luke knew that if he laughed the pain would be unendurable. 'Quite all right,' he whispered. He closed his eyes and drifted away. It seemed to be the only thing left to do. As he sank beneath bosomy wavelets he could hear Jane's voice in the distance. Des-pite rising panic she was keeping her head but she had reverted to Portuguese. *'É uma emergência,'* she said, which he thought meant, 'It is an emergency.' He would have liked to think that she was exaggerating.

SIXTEEN

Luke awoke slowly in what was unmistakably a hospital bed. He had come close to the surface of sleep several times already without quite making it. Even in his half-wakened state he recognized that the hospital was the New Royal in Edinburgh. He seemed to have a side ward to himself. A figure in a white coat had woken him by lifting a corner of his dressing.

The figure, which obviously belonged to a doctor though female and looking impossibly young, said, 'Awake at last? You're a tough old character, aren't you? How old are you?' Her accent was West Highland. She consulted the chart at the foot of the bed. 'I hope I look as young when I'm about a hundred and fifty. They were going to send you back to the ward to wait for a skin graft but you were doing so well under the anaesthetic that they went ahead and finished the job. You'll have a tender donor patch on the other side of your chest but that will soon mend. If all heals the way they expect, that'll be you finished with surgery. How do you feel?'

Luke considered the question. He nearly said 'You tell me,' but that was just the sort of mildly suggestive remark that had got him into trouble, how many times before? Twenty? Fifty? The troubles had been of the sort that other men might dream about but he was too old for that sort of thing, he kept telling himself. 'Sleepy,' he substituted. He closed his eyes with the intention of falling asleep again. 'Sore,' he added. He seemed to have forgotten how to control his voice. His tongue seemed to have developed a life of its own.

'No doubt. But you have an on-demand painkiller. One of the nurses will show you how to use it. There are a whole lot of people, all demanding to visit you and I'm here to decide whether you're fit for visitors yet.'

On the point of asking her to tell the whole lot of people to bugger off and leave him in peace, Luke realized that sleep was receding into the distance and, as memory returned, he was becoming anxious to know just what was going on. 'Whether I'm fit depends on who's waiting to see me. If it's family, well, OK. If it's the police, tell me who.' His control of his tongue seemed to be increasing.

The doctor considered while making a note on a clipboard or possibly filling in a lottery ticket. 'There's certainly family. There's also a lady who says she's police but she has a figure to die for.'

Luke could understand her reservation. A largely sedentary life and one that tended away from healthy eating was not kind to any female figure with a tendency to put on weight. There could be little doubt of the visitor's identity. 'That'll be Honeypot,'he said. He would have liked to leave Detective Chief Inspector Laird until he had spoken with his family but he was sure that she would have other ideas and his male authority would take a knock if she were to overrule him. 'You can let her in but if you hear me raise my voice you'd better come in and find some medical excuse to chuck her out before I do one of us a mischief – me or her, possibly both.'

The doctor smiled noncommittally, evidently torn between loyalty to her patient and to her fellow woman, and left the room. She was soon replaced by Honeypot, who was looking severe. She enquired as to his health and comfort in the shortest terms compatible with elementary courtesy and then leaped to the point. 'I'm obliged to you for delivering those two men into our hands, although I'm quite sure that you turned it into a very profitable trip. I'll even accept that it was our fault rather than yours that the woman slipped through the net. Now tell me all that happened between her arrival at your house and that of the police.'

Luke thought about it. The fog from the anaesthetic was blowing away and he could see where the interview was heading. 'I still don't know how she found her way to my house,' he said, 'but I went in through the French windows. Coming in from sunshine into the dimness, I'd taken a seat in the basket chair in the kitchen before I realized that she was there. She was holding that shotgun and she looked as though she knew how to use it. From what she said, she was blaming me for the arrest of her two colleagues – her lovers, she admitted – and she was not happy.

'She left me in no doubt that she meant to kill me and that she was only postponing the act because she preferred not to give my great-granddaughters warning. She intended to kill them too. I suppose you could say that I chatted her up and I span it out as best I could in the hope that the girls would interrupt. Which they did. By then, I'd made my mind up that no harm was to come to either of them. They must have guessed that something was wrong, perhaps from the sound of our voices – the hearing of the young can be very acute. I could tell by their shadows that they were on the terrace and approaching stealthily. At the last possible moment I threw myself forward and knocked the gun aside, but obviously not quite soon enough. The impact felt exactly as though somebody had hit me hard in the ribs with a hammer and I went down. At the same moment one of the girls – Jane, I'm sure – hit her with a dummy from the launcher. The launcher dummy's made of hard plastic with a metal tube up the middle—'

'And weighs a couple of pounds and gives a hell of a wallop,' said Honeypot impatiently. 'I do know about them. In fact, I was hit by a dummy once during a dog-training session. Go on with the story.'

'The girls dragged the woman outside. That's about it.'

Honeypot's nostrils flared. 'That is not about it, not by a mile,' she said, 'and you know it. I have already had statements from them, remember. And from others.'

'Then you won't need it all over again from me.'

She looked at him in exasperation. 'Do you see any tape recorders here? Or note-books? Even an impartial witness?'

'Not being able to lift my head, I can't see a damn thing.'

'You can see plenty. Take my word for it, there aren't any. If you accept that, you can believe that I'm struggling to give you a fair deal here. The easy way out would be for me to blame you for the woman being assaulted by your family, but I owe you and I feel in part responsible for what's happened to you. Tell me what else you saw and heard.'

Luke could have quarrelled with the *in part*, but he felt too tired for any more argument. 'Very well,' he said. His voice still hurt him so he decided to keep it as short as he reasonably could. 'But remember that I was on the verge of passing out. I couldn't swear to a word of this. My great-grand-daughters arrived in the kitchen doorway. I wasn't going to let them get shot so I took advantage of the distraction. I remember knocking the shotgun aside. That's when it went off. It fell on the floor. They dragged her outside but they came back into the kitchen again, sooner than I expected.' Luke saw a convenient escape route opening up. 'I told them that the woman must on no account be allowed to escape. They told me that they had tied her to a tree. That seemed and still seems to me to accord with the definition of *minimum force necessary*, but I wasn't confident that a couple of young girls could tie knots that an older woman could not untie. Then they told me that even if she did get loose you'd be able to find her very quickly because they had tarred and feathered her. I told them firmly that they should not have done that.'

'No they certainly should not,' Honeypot snapped. 'And they stripped her naked first. You were partly right – she had managed to untie herself. She still wasn't giving up easily. Two constables came across her, trying to break into the garage at Haydock Farm.'

One word seemed out of key. 'Garage?'

'Her first need would be oil so that she could begin to get the tar off. That was two assaults, and even somebody guilty as hell but as yet untried has a right to be protected from attack. It took two policewomen with stiff brushes and a bucket of motor oil all afternoon to get the worst of it off – as much of it as hadn't been left on the seats of the police car. After that, of course, they had to get the oil off and a lot of skin with it. You are not flavour of any passing second in that quarter.'

Luke would have paused to enjoy the mental picture, but the discussion took precedence. 'I don't suppose that I am, and frankly I have no interest in ingratiating myself with that monster. But I hadn't quite finished my statement,' Luke said. 'As I understand it, the law allows the use of what I said – *the minimum force necessary*. The reason that I was so concerned that she mustn't escape was that she had told me that she intended to kill again, in addition to my family and me. And guess who was to be the victim.'

There was a pause. Honeypot blinked at him. 'Me?'

'You.'

After a longer silence she said, 'I can't say that I'm too surprised. This is the second time that I've had the pleasure of putting those two men behind bars.'

'They were both her lovers.'

'I'm still not surprised. That fits with her reputation and explains her hatred. Well, it puts a different complexion on it,' Honeypot said. 'It shouldn't, but as far as I'm concerned it does.'

'I thought it might. She intended to use the girls as hostages to bring you into range.'

'You'd swear to that?'

'Definitely. She told me that much before I was shot, so my memory was still working properly.'

'Let's hope that you don't have to. If she decides to make a fuss I'll have a word with the lady and with the procurator fiscal. Luckily for your granddaughters—'

'Great-granddaughters.'

'Whatever. Luckily for them the assaults took place at your home, in an area where the PF is a much more easy-going character than we get hereabouts. I think I can persuade him not to proceed.'

Despite his relief and the pain, Luke was still curious. 'How?'

'I don't think that there's any need for me to explain the workings of the legal machinery. Just rest assured that I can deal with that gentleman. If the woman tries to proceed against your great-granddaughters I don't think she'll get anywhere.'

Honeypot was replaced at the bedside by Helena, Violet and Jane, each of them anxious and slightly tearful. The nurse had instructed him in the operation of the on-demand painkiller, so he was able to put on an admirable show of courage and he could now speak without feeling that the vibration would cause his chest to implode. 'Honeypot promises to head off the procurator fiscal if there's any question of prosecuting you for your assaults on that woman,' he said, 'and she'll dissuade the woman from bringing a case against you.'

'How did you manage that?' Violet asked. 'The last we saw of that woman, as they were trying to force her into the police car without getting tar and feathers all over themselves, she was screaming that she would drag us through every court in the land.'

'GG can persuade any lady to do anthing,' Jane said proudly. 'That's what they say.'

'Who does?' Helena demanded.

'I think,' Luke said, 'that that's quite enough on that subject.'

'I agree,' Helena said. She felt in her purse. 'Go and get yourself a snack from the machines,' she said. 'You too, Violet.' The two girls left the side ward. 'All the same,' Helena said, 'it was a valid question.'

'I'm not sure of the answer,' Luke said. 'I

told Honeypot, quite truthfully, that the woman told me that she was going to kill her. Kill Honeypot, I mean. I said that that was why I told the girls to make absolutely sure that the woman couldn't get away.'

'And was that the truth?'

'Do you want it to be?'

'No.'

'As far as I was concerned,' said Luke, 'the bitch could have shot Honeypot and welcome. She's been bossing me around, sending me halfway to the equator, putting us all at risk and not so much as a thank you or a lift home. Anyway, she said that she'd persuade the procurator fiscal for our area not to proceed against any of us for assaulting the woman. I can't imagine how.'

Helena smiled as though a new day had dawned. 'Now it all makes sense. It's been a legend and a bit of a standing joke in Newton Lauder, but you never seem to hear any gossip. You've been a great disappointment to me in that respect. Apparently Mr Amish, the PF, made a determined pass at Honeypot after a boozy legal dinner several years ago and she threatened to tell her husband. She still holds it over his head.' She began stroking his hand. 'I stayed with the girls while they made their statements. They both said that you grabbed at the gun to prevent it being turned towards them and that that's how you got shot. Was that true?'

'More or less.'

'Idiot! When they asked me, I said that it was exactly like you.'

Luke thought about trying to sit up but abandoned the idea. 'Who asked you?'

'Reporters,' Helena said. 'And almost everybody else.' She thought that his groan was directly attributable to the mention of reporters but in fact he had jumped at the mention and that had set his wound on fire. He treated himself to another shot of the painkiller. 'A reporter on the local rag,' she resumed, 'had followed up the ambulance call, or else the ambulance crew tipped them off, I don't know which, but he arrived while the girls were still upset and they babbled the story to him and now it's all over the media and there's some talk locally about putting your name forward for a medal.'

Violet and Jane had appeared again at his bedside although he had not seen them return into his limited field of view. 'Ridiculous!' Luke said. 'It's time that you both learned to hold your tongues.' None of his visitors seemed to want to do more than

298

gaze at him admiringly. Luke searched for another subject. 'You two seem to be friends again. No more squabbling over Roddy McWilliam? How did that work itself out? Just so that I know what not to say next time I see him.'

'I don't suppose you'll be seeing much of him from now on,' Violet said. 'We did as you suggested—'

'Don't blame me,' said Luke quickly. 'I don't remember suggesting anything.'

'Well, you did,' said Jane. 'So we went to see him this morning while his mum was out and we asked him which one of us he preferred. You said that he probably wouldn't tell us but he did. He said that he was glad we'd asked the question—'

'Because,' Violet said bravely, 'he thought that we were two very nice girls and very pretty and all that sort of thing and he would always be grateful to Jane for going down the well, but he didn't really fancy either of us much in that sort of way.'

'That,' Luke said carefully, 'is not the impression that Aunt Helena got when she walked into his room unexpectedly.'

Violet flushed. 'I suppose you were bound to hear about that. But nothing happened, not really. Anyway I don't see that you can talk—'

'I haven't uttered a word of criticism,' Luke pointed out, 'although I could and I probably should. But Helena certainly got the impression that some serious fancying was going on.'

'I said something like that,' said Violet. 'And he did apologize very nicely but he said that he couldn't really tell who he fancied until he'd kissed them at least. He said that he really fancied Angie Morrison. He said quite a lot that you wouldn't want to hear, about why he fancied her more than us. That's when I hit him. I know you'll say that it wasn't very ladylike but I was pro-voked. I meant to slap him but it turned into a punch.'

'It was some punch! She was great,' said Jane. 'If I'd known that she could punch like that I'd have been nicer to her. I tried to give him one for luck, but Vi got her arms round me and pulled me off, which was a bit thick when she'd already had the satisfaction. Anyway, he said that he'd always be grateful to me for fishing him out of the well, but he'd come to for a few seconds while I was giving him the kiss of life and the magic just wasn't there, which was a bit thick when you remember that I'd just been sick.'

'All over his head,' Violet reminded her.

'Well yes.'

'And then,' said Violet, 'he had the nerve to ask if we'd give the two of them a lift into Edinburgh. I said that they could bloody well walk.'

'Quite right! I've gone off him in a big way. We talked it over in the car coming through,' Jane said. 'Violet said that she rather fancies Graham Wallace and he's been asking her out, so she thinks she'll go.'

Violet had turned distinctly pink. 'GG's right,' she said. 'You should learn to hold your tongue.'

'His family is quite respectable,' Helena said.

'And he has a younger brother,' Jane said. 'He calls me Pussy because of the well thing. So that's all right. We've nothing left to quarrel about. Life seems rather empty.'

'I expect we'll manage to find something,' said Violet.

'You'll always manage,' Jane said.

Taking great care of his ribs, Luke managed to sigh. 'I shall miss Roddy,' he said. 'I liked the boy.'

Helena gave a ladylike snort. 'See if you still like him after I tell you that he was the one who sang *Just a bonk at twilight*.'

'And I heard him say the thing about a wedding,' Jane said. 'You remember?'

'I remember.'

'Anyway, he's history now,' Helena said.

'That's as well. They tell me that I've missed several days.'

'They kept you under. There were some splinters of bone near an artery and if you'd coughed...'

'I don't think that I want to hear any more on that subject. What's been happening at Kempfield?'

'Mostly, it's been fairly quiet,' Helena said. 'But your camera trap was triggered. Nobody seemed to know what to do about it, so I took the film to Mrs Calder to process and the culprit was that skinny, red-haired boy, Something Jenkins. You remember, he wanted to join but he didn't have any skills or needs or anything else.'

'Hubert,' said Jane.

'That's right. So I went to see his mother. It turned out that she'd been told that she had cancer. Her son had heard that there was a supply of that magic bullet stuff, the cancer cure, in the little room behind the office and he was trying desperately to get hold of some.

'I got hold of Ian Fellowes and he got

Honeypot to help. She's very nice. You don't have to pull faces,' Helena added. 'She thinks you're a real charmer, by the way. Anyway, she went into it and found that the diagnosis came from Dr McGordon just before he scooted abroad. There's nothing wrong with the woman except for a bad case of hypochondria.'